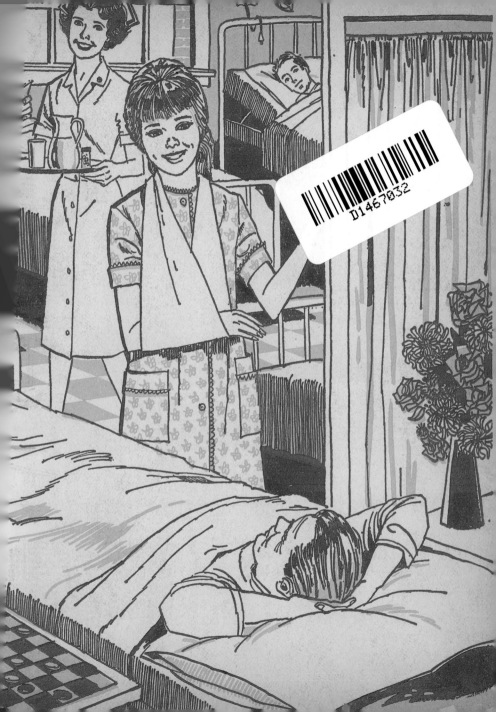

DR. KILDARE

DR. KILDARE

The Magic Key

by William Johnston

Authorized edition based on the
famous M-G-M television series.

illustrated by
Al Andersen and
Jason Art Studio

WHITMAN PUBLISHING COMPANY • Racine, Wis.

Contents

1   Spring!

Clearly, it was spring. Outside Brandon High the noises
in the city streets were more distinct than they had been only
a few days before, no longer hushed by the blanketing
dampness of winter. The single tree in the block, which
rose like a witch's periscope from a small square of earth
that had been left exposed in the sidewalk near the curb,
was showing tiny green buds along its crooked branches.
A Good Humor man pedaled his cart to the school entrance

and dismounted to wait the few minutes until the last class of the day ended and the students came charging out through the doorways. In a small courtyard to the left of the five-story brick school building the hopefuls for the Brandon High baseball team were lined up for inspection by Mr. Caparelli, who doubled as baseball coach and mathematics instructor. The boys who were left over from last season's first team stood to one side of the group. One of them was bunting lazy flies to the others, but there was a glint of eagerness in his eyes and a tautness in his stance that said that he was tempted to swing at the ball and send it whistling like a bullet into the spring air.

Inside the school, in room 204, Mr. Allison was concluding his lecture. He was a spare-framed, mild-faced man. He wondered idly, and half-amusedly, if any of his sophomore students would notice if he abruptly switched the subject from the Federalist Papers to, say, the feeding habits of the Australian kiwi. It was obvious to him that they were much more interested in the presence of spring than in the Federalist Papers.

At any other time, Mr. Allison would have called the students sharply to attention. But today he allowed them their daydreams of the tart, fresh mintiness of the out-of-doors. For the most part they were good pupils, and, to his mind, excellence deserved an occasional reward. Today they could ignore him if they chose, but tomorrow he would crack down. For spring was only beginning its run, and he was here, after all, to teach, not to preside over the breaking up of the educational system.

"So we see that the Federalist Papers were not only an expression of political philosophy, but also that they had considerable literary merit. This is understandable. The authors—Hamilton, James Madison, and John Jay—were men of exceptional. . . ."

At the third desk from the front in the row near the windows, Ginny Dugan sat with her elbows on her desk-top and her chin in her hands. She stared fixedly at Mr. Allison and did not see him at all. Ginny was a pertly pretty girl, with honey-blond hair that was clipped in a ponytail. Her eyes were dark, and as soon as the bell rang ending the class they would flash with a snappy brightness. Even though at the moment she was in a state of suspension, the abundance of energy below the surface was only super-ficially concealed.

Ginny's thoughts were focused on a time that was still several weeks away, when she would compete again for the state baton-twirling championship. In fact, when she would defend her title. Last year she had come away from the competition the winner. She could still recall vividly the instant when she had been proclaimed the victor. She had been standing near the judges' booth, grouped with the other finalists. From where she stood she had been able to see her parents a few yards away—her mother anxiously gnawing on a corner of her scarf, her father sitting hunched forward, looking as if he were wishing that he were some-where else—*any*where else. Then the one judge, the older man with the white hair and the permanent half-smile, had arisen and spoken Ginny's name. It would have been a glorious moment for any of the girls, but for Ginny the glory had been compounded. For one thing, most of the other girls competing were juniors and seniors and Ginny was a freshman. For another, Ginny and her mother were vindicated. For months they had been fighting to convince Ginny's father that the long, hard hours of practicing and hoping were worth the effort, that the championship was important. Now, the cheers proved them right. From this moment on, Ginny was not just another student at Brandon High. She was special.

". . . effect of the Papers began to snowball. They were first printed in New York papers, then reprinted in other papers. And here we see the power of communication. From a small beginning, the ideas incorporated in the Papers, the support for a constitution. . . ."

Bob Carmody, seated on the opposite side of the room from Ginny, doodled figures on the stiff cardboard back of his notebook. If his arithmetic was correct, by saving his allowance during the summer—spending scarcely a penny of it—and then adding it to what he now had in the bank, he would be able to buy his older brother's Ford when his brother left for college in the fall.

But would the prize be worth the sacrifice? And would Ginny put up with it? He had to be fair about it. If he were unable to take her places that cost money, then she would be giving up as much as he. He frankly doubted that her interest in the Ford would be great enough to cause her to accept the sacrifice willingly. She would not have much sympathy for the fact that the Ford was practically a steal at the price his brother was asking and that if he did not take advantage of the opportunity it would most likely be another two years before he would be able to afford a car. On the other hand, if she were asked to sacrifice for a new and more dazzling baton-twirling costume, that would be a different story. But this. . . . Oh, well, he would face the problem later.

Bob stretched out his legs and relaxed. He was a lean and lanky boy, with a crew cut of red hair and pale blue eyes and a peppering of freckles. His gaze drifted toward the windows and settled on Ginny. He smiled contentedly. There were, admittedly, disadvantages to dating the most popular girl in the sophomore class, but they somehow seemed to be outweighed by other aspects. The exact identity of these other aspects eluded him, but he was fully aware that they existed. The whole matter was slightly mysterious; but pleasantly so.

". . . supplementary reading. I would suggest the editions by H. C. Lodge and P. L. Ford. And if you want to go further, there is *The Enduring Federalist,* by C. A. Beard. That's Lodge, Ford, and Beard. If you want to note those names. . . ."

Ellen Morley was seated two places to the right and two

places to the rear of Ginny. She was approximately the same height, five-three, but there the resemblance ended. Ellen was a brunette with green eyes. Her hair hung loosely to her shoulders, clipped at the temples by two matching barrettes. She was somewhat chubbier than she would have wished.

For Ellen, the presence of spring was more of an annoyance than a blessing. It meant that she would begin hating the hours of baton-twirling practice even more than normally. The other girls—except for Ginny—would be out doing things; things that made at least a little bit of sense. But she would be stuck indoors, practicing, practicing. And for what? So she could come in second-best to Ginny again.

Ellen had explained the futility of the practice to her mother. "The point is," she had said, "I don't have a chance. Ginny is so good at it, it's almost absolutely a crime. Why go on?"

"Because people respect people with talent, dear."

"Well, if I'm so talented, why do I always lose?"

"You won't *always* lose. You're improving all the time. And the more you improve, the better you get at it."

Ellen couldn't argue with the logic of this. So she tried

another tack. "But, Mother, I don't really like baton twirling."

"Oh?"

"Well, I don't actually *dis*like it. But there are a lot of other things I'd rather be doing."

"That will change," her mother said. "As soon as you get to be really, really good—expert—you'll love it. Believe me, I know. I could have been a concert pianist if I hadn't stopped practicing."

Ellen was unable to make any sense of this final statement on the matter, but she did not debate the issue any further. She knew from experience that when she pressed her mother for explanations, what she got for her trouble was not an explanation, but one vagary piled on top of another.

The private thoughts of Ginny and Bob and Ellen and the other students were abruptly interrupted by the clanging of the dismissal bell. Room 204 quickly filled with sounds of relief, of notebooks being slapped closed and papers being shuffled restlessly. There were subdued groans as arms and legs stretched and muscles unkinked.

Mr. Allison made a brief announcement.

"We'll continue with the Federalist Papers tomorrow. I have a faint idea that one or two of you weren't paying attention today. So the majority, who were following the lecture so raptly, will have to suffer through a repeat of the high points for the benefit of that inattentive minority."

His comment was rewarded with the laughter it was intended to evoke.

"You may go now."

Most of the students immediately untangled themselves from their desks and began an orderly, if ragged, exodus toward the door. As the door was opened by the first student to reach it, a clamor of voices from the corridor pushed past him into the room. After that, order was abandoned and the stampede was on.

Not all of the pupils joined in the push, however. The half-dozen girls of whom Ginny was the acknowledged leader crowded around her at her desk. There was Ellen Morley, the second-best twirler; Milly Freedburg, who played third violin in the school orchestra; Mary Greccioni, who was taking ballet; Marge Walters, assistant music and dance editor of the school paper; Beth Weiss, the paper's poetry editor; and Joanne Hamilton, who was the occupant of the first chair in the trumpet section of the school band.

At the fringe of this cluster of females sat Oliver Carpenter. Oliver was the class comic. He was waiting for the room to clear so he could explain to Mr. Allison in private why he hadn't turned in a theme paper on the last assignment. The delay did not entirely displease him, however, for he had not yet concocted the explanation he would give. It was Oliver's nature to play life by ear.

The other lingerer, besides Mr. Allison, was Bob Carmody. He remained at his desk, separated from Ginny and her coterie by nearly the width of the room. He passed time by shuffling his books, waiting for Ginny to break away so that, as was the custom, he could walk her home.

As for Mr. Allison, he occupied himself by reading and grading theme papers, and listening with half an ear to the bits of conversation that floated toward him from the circle of girls.

"Don actually wanted to bet on you," Mary was saying to Ginny. "You know, gamble. He was going to be in charge of the whole thing. But when he told his father about it, his father said, 'But suppose she doesn't win? Who will pay off the bets?' So Don decided not to bet. I told him that if he had one loyal bone in his body—one loyal bone—I told him he wouldn't even think about you not winning."

Ginny frowned. "I wouldn't want anyone to bet on me. It would make me nervous."

Marge pooh-poohed this. "You nervous? Last year there wasn't anyone who could even come close to you. All the others, they're the ones who ought to be nervous."

"You're never nervous," Ellen said to Ginny. "I'm the one who gets nervous. When we were out there last year and all those eyes were on us, you were as cool as a block of ice. I was the one who had the shakes. I had the feeling that I was going to hit myself in the back of the head with the baton. The night before the contest, I had a dream that I did, and I thought sure I was going to—right out there in front of everybody." She shrugged. "Not that anyone would have noticed. They were all watching you."

From the fringe, Oliver Carpenter said, "Did you girls hear about the Peace Corps? They're putting on a big recruiting drive for baton twirlers. It's an experiment in exporting democracy. They say that as soon as those people in all those underdeveloped countries have proved that they can live with baton twirlers, they'll be ready for all the other civilized advantages. Like cars that automatically fall apart as soon as the new models come out. And boxes of cornflakes that have more air than cornflakes."

There was some laughter—but only because Oliver was fairly good-looking.

"Your trouble is, Oliver," Milly said, "you're too old for your age. You don't enjoy anything."

This got a bigger laugh.

"Give us a solo on your third-violin." Oliver grinned.

The girls closed him out of the circle.

"Will you be ready for the contest?" Ginny asked Ellen. "If we could take both first *and* second this year, we could probably get a lot of publicity or something for the school. Remember last year? Remember those twins who competed? They were on television."

"The only way that will happen to us is if we all of a sudden become twins," Ellen said. "I try. I practice and I practice. But I'm just not you."

"Your mother says you're improving all the time," Mary said sympathetically.

"The trouble with my mother is, she loves me."

Ginny began collecting her books. This was the signal that the discussion was ended, that Ginny now intended to transfer her attention to Bob Carmody.

By twos, the other girls departed. Then Ginny got to her feet and smiled across the room at Bob. He smiled in return, and began extricating his lankiness from the confining design of the desk.

Oliver Carpenter grimaced, realizing that the moment of truth was at hand.

At the same instant there was a loud cracking sound from outside as the boy in the courtyard gave in to temptation and leaned the bat into the baseball.

At the sound, Ginny half-turned toward the windows. And as she did there was a sudden crash and splintering of glass. The baseball bounced off the far wall of the classroom. Ginny screamed and dropped her books. Blood spurted from a gash in her right forearm. She screamed again, hysterically now. "Bob! Help me!"

Bob Carmody leaped up and darted through the maze of desks.

Mr. Allison, too, rushed toward Ginny.

Oliver, stunned, touched his hand to the scratch on his cheek, then looked at the hand and saw a watery red wetness. He stared, fascinated by the sight of his own blood.

"Bob! Help me!"

Bob reached Ginny and caught her just as she lost consciousness.

"Put her down right here," Mr. Allison commanded, indicating the floor. He whipped off his jacket, then his shirt. "Go down to the office," he ordered. "Get an ambulance. That cut is deep."

Bob ran from the room.

Mr. Allison tore his shirt into strips. Then he knelt beside Ginny and began binding the wound. The cloth quickly reddened. A pale bluish-grayness came into Ginny's face. Her breathing became shallow and irregular.

"Get something to cover her," Allison snapped at Oliver.

"What?"

"A blanket. Something. Anything. Jump!"

Oliver smiled feebly. "A blanket?"

"She's going into shock. We have to keep her warm. Move, will you! Move!"

Oliver shook his head, like a puppy shaking off water

after a swim, then, in possession of himself again, dashed off.

Soon the wail of a siren was heard—from a distance, but drawing nearer.

2   Emergency

In the surgical section of the Emergency Ward at Blair General Hospital, a patient, a middle-aged male, was having an accidental head wound closed. He had been given only a local anesthetic, so he was vaguely aware of where he was and what was happening. His hands, protruding from the sleeves of the hospital gown, opened and closed, slowly keeping time to some rhythm that was pulsing in his mind.

On one side of the operating table was Dr. Wilson Everleigh, the chief resident (surgery) on duty. Everleigh was a short, dark, bulky man in his early thirties. He had been on duty for ten hours straight. Below the rim of his skull cap, bright little beads of perspiration glistened, reflecting the brilliance of the overhead lights. With needle and nylon thread he was stitching together the edges of the wound in the patient's scalp. The procedure was fairly routine, and working a ten-hour tour was not uncommon for Dr. Everleigh, so the slightly sick look on his face begged for a fuller explanation.

Facing Dr. Everleigh across the operating table was Dr. James Kildare, an intern, who had been assigned to the service a few weeks before. Kildare was tall and blond and somewhat boyish-looking. His attention was partly on the work that Everleigh's fingers were performing and partly on the distress he observed in the doctor's expression.

To Everleigh's right stood the scrub nurse, Miss Wyatt. She looked, and was, as sure and efficient as an electronic computer. A few steps back from the table, behind Dr. Kildare, was the circulating nurse, Miss Emerson. She was a few years younger than the scrub nurse and had a softer, more vulnerable look about her.

Everleigh straightened and groaned, as if his muscles had rebelled; then he knotted the thread.

Miss Wyatt slapped a scissors-like instrument into his hand. He snipped loose the free ends of the thread.

"Are you tired?" Kildare asked.

Everleigh glared. Then he turned to Miss Wyatt. "That'll do it."

"Yes, Doctor."

Everleigh headed for the door and Kildare followed him. Behind them, the nurses wheeled the table toward another exit, the one which led to the recovery room.

In the small office outside the operating room, Everleigh dropped into a chair and stretched his stubby legs and groaned again. He pulled off his cap and stripped off his gloves. Then he closed his eyes.

Kildare remained standing—and watching. "Are you all right, Wilson?"

"I'm coming down with something," Everleigh answered. He smiled without opening his eyes. "I guess I picked the right spot for it. Call me a doctor, will you?"

Kildare laughed. "Do you have any idea what it is?"

"I'm a surgeon, I don't diagnose aches and pains."

"You better call a relief."

"Yes." Everleigh sighed. He sat up. "Hold down the fort. I'll see who's available." He started to rise.

But he dropped back into the chair, looking pained, as Miss Wyatt came hurrying into the room. "No, not another one," he said.

"A young girl," Miss Wyatt announced briskly. "Arm wound. Broken glass. She's in shock. They're bringing her in now."

Everleigh dragged himself up and motioned to Kildare. He led the way through the operating room to the scrub room. There, he dropped the gloves and soiled gown he had removed earlier into a waste container, then moved on to the sinks. Kildare stripped off his own gloves and gown, and joined Everleigh.

With stiff-bristled brushes, the two doctors scrubbed their fingers, between the fingers, their wrists, and up the arms. When they had finished they dipped their hands into antiseptic, then stood while Miss Wyatt replaced the soiled gowns with fresh ones. After that came new gloves, taken from sealed plastic packets.

As Everleigh and Kildare entered the operating room, Ginny, still unconscious, was being lifted by two interns from a stretcher to the table. She was wrapped tightly in hospital blankets. Her face was still a bluish-gray.

"Do we have her blood type?" Everleigh asked one of the interns.

"Type B. There was a teacher there who got it from the school records. Pretty bright guy. He had her wrapped in some blankets he got from the school nurse's office. She was cut by flying glass from a broken window. Some kid hit a baseball through it."

"Yeah, okay, okay." Everleigh pointed to Miss Wyatt. "Blood and heat packs." He turned to Kildare. "Manometer. Let's have a reading on the pressure."

Miss Wyatt and Kildare hurried away.

"Get her out of that straitjacket," Everleigh said to Miss Emerson.

The nurse began unwrapping the blankets from Ginny.

The two interns who were assigned to the ambulance departed.

When Ginny was free of the blankets, Miss Emerson began cutting her clothes from her.

Everleigh waited distractedly. He blinked his eyes, then closed them and shook his head as if he were trying to clear his mind.

Kildare returned with the manometer. He glanced at Everleigh and made a face of concern. Then he turned his attention to his work and began taking Ginny's blood pressure.

"Kildare," Everleigh said suddenly.

"Yes?" He kept his eyes on his work.

"You're it. I'll get a relief down here as soon as I can. Can you handle it?"

"It'll be all right."

"You get that blood into her fast."

"Right."

Everleigh turned away and walked groggily to the exit.

Miss Wyatt arrived with the heat packs. She looked around for Dr. Everleigh.

"Let's go, let's go," Kildare said sharply.

Instantly, Miss Wyatt responded. She began nesting Ginny in the heat packs. "The blood is on the way," she said.

Miss Emerson was waiting with an antiseptic sheet, ready

to cover Ginny once the packs were in place.

Kildare disengaged the manometer and put it aside. Then he began cutting the temporary bandage from Ginny's arm.

Miss Emerson fitted the sheet into place, leaving the arm uncovered.

The door that led to the recovery room opened and an orderly entered with the containers of whole blood. Miss Wyatt began setting up the transfusion apparatus.

Inspecting the wound, Kildare said, speaking more to himself than the nurses, "It severed the skeletal muscle." Then, turning to Miss Emerson, he said, "I want a local."

"Yes, Doctor." She darted away.

"Ready with the blood." It was Miss Wyatt speaking.

Kildare moved to the other side of the table and bared Ginny's left arm. He held out a hand and Miss Wyatt slapped a scalpel into it. Kildare made a short, quick incision, then passed the scalpel back to Miss Wyatt. She placed the tube from the transfusion apparatus into his hand. At the end of the tube was a slender, delicate needle. Kildare inserted the needle into the vein.

Across the table, Miss Emerson was busy injecting the anesthetic.

Miss Wyatt activated the transfusion mechanism. Whole blood began entering Ginny's veins through the tube.

Kildare and Miss Wyatt circled the ends of the table, with the nurse pushing the instrument cart in front of her. Miss Emerson stepped back and Kildare took her place. "Keep a constant check on the pressure," Kildare said to her.

Kildare bent over the wound. He studied it for a second, then held out a hand. "Retractor."

Miss Wyatt slapped a clawlike instrument into his palm. He fitted it to one edge of the wound, pulling back the flesh and underlying tissue.

"Retractor."

Again there was a slap against his glove. He fitted the second retractor to the opposite edge of the wound, so that now he had working space.

"Pressure rising," Miss Emerson reported.

Kildare reached. Miss Wyatt reacted.

With the bulbed instrument she had handed him, Kildare flushed out the wound with an antiseptic solution.

"Rising, Doctor."

A faint touch of color appeared in Ginny's cheeks.

The suturing began. Kildare took stitch after minute stitch in the muscle, closing it with a thread that in time would dissolve.

Miss Emerson reported periodically on the blood pressure and gradually the effects of the transfusion showed up in deeper patches of pink in Ginny's face.

Time plodded on. The closing of the severed muscle was completed; then Kildare began sewing together the severed ligaments and tendons.

Smiling, Miss Emerson reported, "One-twenty systolic, eighty diastolic."

Kildare grinned but he did not look up. He finished off a suture, tied off the thread, then straightened. He and Miss Wyatt moved to the opposite side of the table. He disengaged the tube from the vein. Miss Wyatt took away the transfusion apparatus.

Ginny's breathing was now quiet and even. Her face was a blushing pale color.

Kildare closed the incision he had made for the tube, then returned to the primary operation. The stitching began again. Another half hour passed. Finally, he tied off the last stitch. He stepped back and arched his spine, straining against the tenseness.

Miss Emerson moved in and began bandaging the now-closed wound.

"I wonder what happened to that relief?" Kildare said curiously.

Then a rare thing happened. Miss Wyatt smiled. "You didn't need any help, Doctor," she said. The smile immediately disappeared.

Kildare grinned. "Keep the check on the pressure in Recovery," he said to Miss Emerson.

"Yes, Doctor."

Kildare headed toward the door that led to the small outer office. Miss Wyatt and Miss Emerson wheeled the table toward the exit that led to the recovery room.

Stepping into the office, Kildare suddenly halted and stared. He now knew why the relief had not arrived. Dr. Everleigh was slumped in a chair, unconscious.

Kildare hurried to him and felt his pulse. It was weaker than normal, but not dangerously so. He picked up the phone on the desk and dialed an extension. When the voice of a nurse came on, he said, "This is Dr. Kildare in Emergency. I want a diagnostician—fast."

"Yes, Doctor."

Kildare paced nervously while he waited.

Then Miss Wyatt entered the office. "The Dugan girl's parents are waiting, Doctor," she said. "Will you—" She saw Everleigh slumped in the chair.

"He apparently came out here and then passed out," Kildare said. "I've sent for a diagnostician. I want to find out for sure what it is. He may have infected the patients."

She nodded. "Do you want to talk to the Dugan girl's parents now?"

"Who?"

"The Dugan girl. Virginia Dugan. You just sewed up her wound."

"Oh . . . oh, sure. Ask them to wait a minute, will you please? I want to find out about Dr. Everleigh first."

"Yes, Doctor." She left the room.

A few moments later, Dr. Carl Hornquist, head of the diagnostic section, arrived. He was an older man, in his late fifties. His examination of Everleigh was brief. "A virus," he said. "How long has he been on duty?"

"Over ten hours."

"No wonder he passed out. Well, we'll have to get him

to bed, and—" He saw Kildare's dark look. "Do you have something hanging? I can take care of this."

"He's handled a number of patients; I wonder if he's infected any of them."

"It isn't serious if he did. But they better have injections anyway."

"I'll see to it."

Hornquist picked up the phone and dialed and then said, "I'll get a stretcher down here for Everleigh. You go on."

Relieved, Kildare returned to the operating room. He gave orders to Miss Wyatt for medication for the patients with whom Everleigh had had contact.

"Now then," he said, "where are the parents?"

"Reception Two, Doctor."

"Thank you."

Kildare left the operating room, passed through the small office where two orderlies were lifting Everleigh to a stretcher, then entered the corridor and headed for the reception area.

3   Only the Beginning

Reception Two, a much smaller room than Main Reception, was located a few yards down the corridor from Emergency. It was a boxy sort of room, painted a light blue, with a large window looking out onto the corridor. The furnishings were adequate but far from luxurious. There was a tubular-steel couch and two chairs, all with foam rubber cushions. At one end of the couch was a small table, and there was another small table between the two chairs. The tables were cluttered with magazines and each one held an ashtray. A number of framed prints of city scenes, like small windows to the outside world, decorated the walls. In one corner was a water cooler.

Ginny's father, George Dugan, was sitting at the end of the couch near the table. He was slouched down in the seat, scowling, and there was a dead cigar clamped tightly between his teeth. George Dugan was a large, heavy-shouldered man. He had once played semi-professional football. Now he owned a trucking company that specialized in transporting steel plate and beams from the mills to construction sites. The company was quite prosperous. George Dugan had made it so by keeping it lean; by making each of the many steps of the operation as slickly efficient as possible. George had a monstrous distaste for waste and frills.

Sitting up stiffly in one of the chairs was Mary Dugan, Ginny's mother. Mary was a tall, chic, slender woman. She was dressed in a dark-blue linen sheath. Conscious of her husband's respect for simplicity, her only accessory, save for her purse, was a single strand of pearls. The seeking for simplicity, too, had dictated the severe French knot into which her auburn hair had been styled.

There was a moistness in Mary's eyes. A wrong word would have triggered the tears. Her hands were in her lap and her fingers were locked so tightly together that the knuckles were white. She had long ago chewed away most of her lipstick.

George looked at his wife and his natural scowl deepened. "Relax," he said gruffly.

"Where *is* that doctor?"

"You heard the nurse; he's on his way. Take it easy, Mary. Ginny's okay. You heard what the nurse said. Relax."

"Maybe there's a complication."

"Nonsense. What was it? Just a little cut on the arm. That teacher who called—what was his name?—he told you that—just a little cut on the arm. And the nurse said that it's all fixed up and Ginny's resting easy. What more do you want?"

Mary untangled her fingers and sat back, slightly less tense. "Thank the Lord it wasn't her face. We can be grateful for that."

"Sure."

"You don't realize how bad it could have been. When

I think about what *could* have happened. All that flying glass. She could have been scarred for life. Her face, I mean. She—" The tears, held in check so long, now escaped. She opened her purse and dug into it for a tissue.

George groaned. "What *could* have happened doesn't count," he said crossly. "The fact is, she has a little cut on her arm. There won't be any scar. It'll go away. Remember when that steel plate got away from that fellow and I got that scrape on the leg? It was gone, disappeared, within a week or so. Come on now, knock off the tears."

Mary dabbed at her eyes with the tissue. "Scars don't matter to men. But a girl with a scar, and a girl Ginny's age, right now when she's just beginning to—"

The door opened and a tall, blond, smiling young man entered the room.

"Mr. and Mrs. Dugan? I'm Dr. Kildare."

George pushed himself to his feet, nodding acknowledgment. "Glad to know you. The nurse said you'd be along."

"Hello, Doctor," Mary said, remaining seated. "Was the nurse right? Is Ginny—is everything. . . ."

"She's fine," Kildare said. "She's in Recovery right now."

"May we see her?"

"If you want to. But she's unconscious. She'll be unconscious for another few hours."

"We'd like to see her anyway," Mary said. "I just want to reassure myself."

"Of course." Kildare smiled. "Come along."

He led the way out of the reception room and down the corridor and around the corner to the corridor entrance to the recovery room. "She'll probably look a little pale to you," he said, opening the door. "She'd lost a lot of blood and gone into shock. We had to give her transfusions. But, if all goes well, she'll pretty much have her normal color back by tomorrow."

There was a sharp intake of breath.

"What do you mean, 'if all goes well'?" Mary asked frightenedly.

"What? Oh . . . nothing specific. There's no reason to believe that all won't go well."

Mary had stopped in the doorway. "Are you sure, Doctor? Are you positively sure?"

"Mary," George scolded, "that's just a figure of speech. If all goes well. I say it all the time. Will you *relax?* Ginny's fine. She's fine, isn't she, Doctor?"

"Considering what happened—the shock—she's in excellent condition," Kildare said.

Mary chewed at her lips. "Well . . . all right."

They entered the recovery room and Kildare took them to the bed on which Ginny was still lying. The room was dimly lit. A duty nurse was sitting at a desk near the passageway between this room and the operating room.

Ginny was covered up to the neck with a sheet. Her eyes were closed. The clip that had held her blond hair in a ponytail had been removed and her hair was now hanging free, making a golden pillow for her head.

"She looks so lonely," Mary whimpered.

"No more lonely than she ever looked before when she was asleep," George said exasperatedly.

"Is the wound awful?" Mary asked.

Kildare lifted the sheet and showed her the bandaged arm. "Fairly attractive, I'd say." He smiled. "It's what's being worn this season in all the best hospitals—sterile gauze."

Mary smiled thinly. "When will she be conscious again?"

"As I said, in a few hours. She'll regain consciousness and she'll feel very weak and very tired. She'll want to sleep. So it will be morning before you'll be able to talk to her."

"And you're sure there are no complications?"

"At the moment, none whatever."

Mary still did not seem wholly satisfied.

"I'll show you the way back to the reception room," Kildare said, moving away.

The Dugans followed. At the door, Mary took one last look at her daughter. She sniffled and dabbed at her eyes, then accompanied Kildare and her husband into the corridor.

As they walked toward the reception room, George said to Kildare, "A little thing like this, a little cut, I guess it won't keep her in the hospital very long, will it, Doctor?"

"If it were only a little cut, it wouldn't," Kildare replied. "But this was somewhat more than that. A skeletal muscle was severed. I had to stitch it together. Even so, though, I see no reason why she shouldn't be able to leave in a few days. I'll know better tomorrow, after I've had a chance to examine the wound again."

"A week maybe?"

"Less than that."

"It's important, you see, Doctor," Mary said, "because Ginny has to keep up her practice. The contest is only a few weeks away."

Kildare looked at her blankly.

George smiled dryly. "Our daughter's a baton-twirling champion," he said to Kildare. "Don't tell me that you don't keep up-to-date on the latest in the stick-throwing game."

Kildare laughed. "I'm afraid not."

"Can't imagine that," George said. "The fate of the whole civilized world depends on how Ginny does in the contest, you know. I don't see how a fellow could claim to be very interested in his fellowman and not know a thing like that."

"All right, George," Mary said sharply.

"Other people," George went on, "they worry about the state of the economy, taxes, the gold flow, integration, and the like. Us, we live and breathe baton throwing. Fascinating business. What it is, you take this stick, about yea long, and you whirl it around. Then, when you get real good at it, you throw it up in the air and catch it. And to be able to do this very essential thing, you have to practice.

Hours. That's what Ginny does. Believe it or not."

"She won't be practicing for a while," Kildare said.

Mary abruptly halted. "What do you mean?"

The two men stopped, too. George looked annoyed.

"I didn't mean permanently," Kildare said. "I just meant that she won't be able to use her hand that strenuously for a while—a matter of a few weeks. As I mentioned before, the skeletal muscle was severed and had to be sewn. Strenuous use of the hand and arm might tear loose the stitches."

"But the contest," Mary protested.

"Well . . . when is it?"

"Less than a month away."

Kildare shook his head. "No, she won't be able to enter it."

Mary took a step toward him. "Doctor, you don't understand. Ginny is the state champion. It's very important. I know George doesn't think it is. But it is. Very important."

"I'm sorry," Kildare said, frowning. "If you want to put your daughter in that contest, there's nothing I can do to stop you. But it would be wrong. The muscle will not be completely healed." He smiled. "I don't think there will be much of a problem, though. Your daughter won't feel like competing. Her arm and hand will be stiff for a while."

"That won't stop her," George said.

"I think it will. She couldn't very well do her best with stiff fingers, could she?"

Mary began to cry again. She shook her head tragically. "This is awful. Just awful."

"Oh, sure," George said. "She'll probably have to spend her time reading or some horrible thing like that for a couple weeks. Well, that's show business, as they say—on top of the heap one day, a has-been the next."

Mary looked at him coldly, then turned to Kildare again. "Doctor, isn't there some chance that she might be fully recovered in time for the contest? You said she could leave here in a few days. It would seem to me—"

"I meant that she could do her recovering at home."

"Doctor, please, try to understand. I realize that baton twirling isn't . . . well, isn't the most important thing in the world. Not in itself anyway. But there are other things that are connected with it. Because of being the best, Ginny is a very popular girl at school. You know how youngsters are. Things like that are important to them. Not that it matters to me—really. I'm thinking about Ginny. She's used to being fussed over. And to suddenly lose that . . . it's going to be extremely difficult for her."

"Nonsense," George said. "Ginny's a sensible girl. She won't miss all that fiddle-faddle. As a matter of fact, this is probably a good thing. She'll get that baton-twirling business out of her system. Maybe she'll spend her time doing something worthwhile."

"Dr. Kildare," Mary went on, "if you could just—"

"Mary!" George broke in. "The doctor doesn't care about this. It isn't his concern. We'll talk about it later."

She sighed and, for a brief instant, looked at her husband belligerently. Then she surrendered, left the men, and walked on down the corridor toward the elevators.

"I apologize for this family stuff," George said to Kildare. "But you know how women are. Once they get an idea in their heads, there's nothing short of blasting that can get it out. They're unreasonable. I've stood my ground on this stick-throwing rubbish, fighting it all the way, but they're stubborn, they won't give an inch." He lifted his hands in a gesture of resignation. "What can a man do?"

Kildare smiled noncommittally.

George put out a hand. "Thanks, Doctor. We'll see you tomorrow probably."

Kildare took the hand. "Yes, I'll be around."

George turned and walked to where his wife was waiting.

Kildare watched them speculatively as they stood together at the elevators. He saw them speak briefly to each other and observed that Mary was crying again and that George was biting off his words. Then he shrugged and returned to the small office outside the operating room.

Outside the hospital, the Dugans got into a cab. After George had given the driver the address, he settled back and turned to his wife who was seated as far away from him as she could get.

"I guess you're mad," he said.

She remained silent.

"I didn't see any point in hashing out our troubles in front of that doctor," George said. "It's none of his business."

"I know," she said repentantly. "I'm sorry."

"Well, forget it. Honestly, Mary, I stick with what I said—this is probably a good thing. Not the cut, I don't

mean that, but getting Ginny out of that contest. You know how worked up she gets. That's not good. To see her out there, you'd think she was cool as a cucumber. But, you and me, we know different. It's too important to her. If it was something that had some kind of value, I'd say fine. But this. It's nonsense. Pure nonsense, that's all."

"It isn't nonsense to her."

"It should be."

"Why? Because you can't understand it?"

George groaned. "Okay, okay."

"How many times do I have to explain it? It isn't the baton twirling itself that matters so much, it's what goes with it. It's made Ginny popular, and that *is* important. Don't you remember how it was to be a youngster, George? Being popular was everything."

"Not for me."

"You just don't remember."

"Maybe what the trouble is, maybe I just don't remember how it was for you when you were a youngster. Was there something you wanted for yourself when you were young and you didn't get it? If that's the case, I think it's wrong to try to get it for Ginny now. Let her lead her own life, let her have her own wants, not yours."

"What I wanted as a youngster has nothing to do with it," Mary said defensively. "Except that, having been a young girl myself, I know what is important to young girls. That's your trouble, George. You've never been a young girl."

George laughed. "I can't argue with that, hon."

"So you can't understand."

"Well, the problem's over and done with anyway. You heard the doctor. She won't be baton twirling for a while. And, unless I miss my guess, that'll be the end of it. She'll miss a season and she'll grow out of it. She'll get interested in something else, something with some value. So—" he grinned broadly, "—no problem."

Mary turned away and looked out the window of the cab. "My guess is that the problem is just beginning."

"No, we've had the last of it. I'll lead her along into something new, some new interest. Golf maybe. Good exercise. Or checkers. I used to play a championship game of checkers—you probably didn't know that. Or something practical. They're doing some pretty fascinating things in construction these days. Reinforced concrete, for one thing.

I've got some articles on it that she could read while she's in the hospital."

Mary shook her head pityingly.

He grinned again. "Only kidding, hon, only kidding."

4   A Matter of Opinion

Ginny awakened to a sound—a soft padding sound. She opened her eyes and through the first haze of consciousness saw a movement of white. Gradually her vision cleared. The white became a nurse, a pleasant-faced girl in her middle twenties. Ginny was then able to identify the sound; it was made by the rubber soles of the nurse's shoes as she pushed around a small cart on which there were a number of beakers and jars and shiny metal objects.

Ginny turned her head slightly to observe the room. There were two windows. The sun was slanting in through the partly opened blinds, making a pattern of bars on the floor. There were two tubular-steel chairs near the windows. To the right of her bed was a metal stand, and on it a metal container that held a cluster of yellow chrysanthemums.

"Hello."

The nurse, smiling, was now standing beside Ginny's bed.

"Hello," Ginny replied. She was startled by the feebleness of her own voice.

"I'm Miss Walker. How do you feel?"

"A little woozy."

"Well, that's natural."

"Am I all right?"

The nurse laughed lightly. "You're fine. Dr. Kildare will be in soon. He'll tell you whatever you want to know."

"I remember the broken window," Ginny said. "And then—" She tried to move her right arm, which was covered by the sheet, and winced. "It was my arm that was hurt, wasn't it? I remember that. It kind of stings."

"You had some stitches taken in it," Miss Walker said.

"Dr. Kildare will be in to tell you about it." She went to the cart and returned with a thermometer. "Open."

Lying quietly with the tip of the thermometer under her tongue, Ginny strained her mind to remember more. She could recall the sudden shattering of the window, seeing the rush of blood on her arm, screaming for Bob. But after that there was a stretch of vagueness. Her next recollection was of a dimly lighted room; a room somewhat like this one. There was a woman there, a woman in white, and the woman had spoken to her, but Ginny could not remember what she had said. Then a needle. Yes, she had caught a glimpse of the needle. Then nothing. Nothing until now.

Miss Walker took the thermometer from Ginny and held it up to the light.

"Where was I—in the hospital, I mean—where was I before I came here?" Ginny asked.

"In Operating and in Recovery." She took the instrument to the cart and deposited it in one of the beakers.

"I remember a woman and a needle."

"That was probably the nurse in Recovery. You regained consciousness and she gave you a sedative."

Ginny felt a little better having the mystery cleared up.

"This seems like a lot of fuss—" she began.

She was interrupted by the door opening. A tall, blond young man entered. "Good morning." He smiled, closing the door behind him. "I'm Dr. Kildare."

"Oh, yes," Ginny smiled, "you're the one."

"The one?"

Miss Walker spoke up. "I told her that you are her doctor. She's been trying to remember what happened."

"I see." Kildare got a chair from near the windows and brought it to Ginny's bedside. "Your parents are waiting to see you," he said. "They arrived just a few minutes ago. I want to take a look at the stitches, then I'll send them in."

"I'll bet they're worried, aren't they? Mother especially."

"Well, they're not taking it as well as the patient. But that's normal." He turned toward the nurse. "Miss Walker, will you bring the cart over, please?" Then to Ginny, he said, "Do you have any pain in the arm?"

"It stings a little."

"That's expected." He lifted the sheet and uncovered the arm, then took a pair of scissors from the cart, which Miss Walker had wheeled to the bedside, and began removing the bandage. "Have you used your hand at all yet?" he said to Ginny, his hands working carefully.

"No, I've just been lying here."

"I mean have you manipulated the fingers, opened and closed the hand?"

She shook her head.

"Don't be afraid to. Be easy with it for a while, though." He dropped the bandage into the waste container on the lower shelf of the cart. "Try it now. Move your fingers."

A touch of exertion showed on Ginny's face. "They're stiff," she said.

Kildare nodded, unperturbed. "All right, forget it for now. But, during the day, try again. The stiffness is natural; a muscle in your arm was severed and I had to join it. We don't want the stiffness to continue, however. So, every once in a while, try moving your fingers again. But easy."

Ginny looked at him a little frightenedly. "Doctor, will my hand be all right?"

"Yes." He smiled. "Don't worry about it. You'll be going home in a couple days."

She sighed relievedly. "You said to be careful with my fingers. I wondered."

"I just don't want you to pull those stitches loose."

"Oh." Ginny sighed again in relief.

Kildare applied medication to the wound, then re-bandaged it. "I'll send your parents in now," he said, getting up and carrying the chair back to the windows. "And I imagine you could probably use some breakfast, too."

"I'm not especially hungry."

He looked at her with mock severity. "Eat. Doctor's orders."

She laughed. "Yes, Doctor."

Kildare smiled again, then left.

"He's nice, isn't he?" Ginny said to Miss Walker.

"Ummm—very attractive. Now, what will it be? Mush or soft-boiled eggs?"

Ginny made a face.

"That's the soft-boiled eggs look," Miss Walker said. And, wheeling the cart in front of her, she departed.

Alone, Ginny lifted her arm, as if she were giving an Indian sign, and looked closely at the bandage. It was neatly done. What movie was it where the heroine had worn a bandage? An old war movie on television. But then, *her* bandage had been around her head—some sort of a bullet wound or something. Still, an arm bandage was probably preferable. If you had your head all wrapped up, how could you wash your hair?

Ginny smiled to herself. The bandage did not displease her. In a way, it looked sort of—well, tragic.

She peered at her fingers. They looked perfectly all right. She tried to close them and felt the twinge again in the area of the wound. But that would go away. A matter of time. Let's see, she would be going home in a couple days, and if she could go home there was probably no reason why she couldn't also go back to school. By then the sting would be gone and—

The door opened.

Mary Dugan appeared first. She was smiling—but thinly, showing that she was determined to be cheerful despite her true feelings. Behind her was Ginny's father. George Dugan wore an expression of righteous irritation.

Mary made a clucking sound. "Darling, your hair," she said vexedly, hurrying to the bed. "It's all undone. It looks frightful."

George lifted a hand in salute. "Hi, sweetie." He closed the door, then stood.

"George, bring me one of those chairs," Mary said. She

had already taken a comb from her purse. "Why didn't someone do something about your hair?" she said to Ginny. "I suppose they expect you to take care of yourself—and with your arm that way." She cluck-clucked again.

"I just woke up, Mother."

George placed the chair beside the bed. "She looks okay to me," he said.

"When you're feeling horrible, it always helps to look nice," Mary said, sitting down and beginning to pull the comb through Ginny's hair.

"I don't feel horrible, Mother. Just a little weak."

Mary stopped combing. "Then the doctor didn't tell you."

"Tell me what?"

"Now, wait a minute," George said. "It's not as bad as all that. In fact, it's not bad at all. It's a good thing, if you want my opinion."

"Tell me *what?*" Ginny repeated, her voice rising.

"Well, that you won't be able to compete in the contest," her mother replied. "We assumed that he'd told you. I don't know why he didn't. It's unfair. He should have told you the first thing."

"Maybe it didn't seem that important to him," George said brusquely. "He probably has a couple other things on his mind; people with real problems."

"He didn't say anything like that to me," Ginny said to her mother. There was an undercurrent of panic in her tone now. "He said I could go home soon—in a few days. I thought— Are you sure? You must be wrong. He said that I could go home."

"Yes, dear, you *can* go home. But you can't be in the contest. It's because of the stitches. You see, you might— what was it he said?—you might break them or something like that. It's all very silly, if you ask me, but you know how doctors are."

"What's silly about it?" George asked. "If she broke open the stitches, she'd be right back in here."

"Well, that's what the doctor thinks, anyway," Mary said. "I don't know; I'm not an expert on it like your father."

"Me? It's not me. The doctor said that, not me. He's the expert."

Ginny's distress was growing. "But, did you explain to him?" she said to her mother.

"I told him," Mary said. "I told him how important it is. But . . . you know doctors."

"Well, now," George said, "let's just discuss that. Let's just see how important it is. What's more important—for Ginny to get out there and throw that stick around or for the wound to heal? If we're talking about what's important, let's just consider that. Which is? I ask you—which is?"

Mary began combing Ginny's hair again. "We're not arguing with you, George," she said coolly.

"Good. Then that's it. Let's hear no more about it."

Tears came into Ginny's eyes.

George turned away and went to the windows and stood with his back to the room.

Mary tugged the knots out of Ginny's hair.

"That kid—what's-his-name?—came around last night," George said.

"Bob," Mary explained to Ginny. "He wanted to find out how you were. He wants to come to the hospital to visit you. Some of your other friends, too. I told him it would probably be all right."

"Did you tell him about the other?" Ginny asked tearfully. "Did you tell him?"

"About the contest? Yes."

From the windows, George said, "I thought we weren't going to talk about that anymore."

"She asked."

"Okay. Let's drop it. Let's just drop it, that's all."

Mary searched in her purse, then came up with a rubber band and twisted it around Ginny's hair to make a ponytail.

George faced back into the room. "Now look, hon," he said to Ginny, "as far as I'm concerned, the subject is dead. But there's one more thing I want to say. This is ridiculous. I'll tell you this, if I had a man working for me and he moped around about a ridiculous thing like this, I'd give him the boot—and fast."

He got no reply. Ginny blinked back the tears. Mary looked at her husband tight-lipped and disapprovingly.

"So that's it," George said gruffly. "No more. The subject is closed." He scowled uncomfortably. "How are you feeling?" he said. "We haven't even asked you."

"A little weak is all."

"And where they sewed you up, how's that?"

"Well—it stings a little. And I can't move my fingers."

"That'll pass. The doctor said your arm would be a little

stiff for a while." He suddenly looked concerned. "Say, what about your schoolwork? I wonder if we'll have to get a tutor in or if you'll be able to go back to classes." He turned to his wife. "We'll have to mention that to the doctor and see what he says."

"Maybe the school could send my homework to the house," Ginny said.

"Well, we'll see. If the doctor says you can go back, there's no reason to hibernate at home."

"I might hurt my arm—open up the stitches, I mean," Ginny said. "Sometimes the pushing in the hallways gets pretty treacherous."

George grinned. "Then stay out of the hallways. You want to go back to school, don't you? I'd think you would, with that fancy bandage you've got there to show off. I remember when I was a kid, I used to sometimes stick a little piece of adhesive tape to my forehead just for the heck of it. I didn't have a cut or anything, understand. Just to get some attention."

"I'm thinking of my arm," Ginny said. "Dr. Kildare said to be careful with it. I think he's worried about it."

George looked at his wife, then back at Ginny. "He

didn't seem worried when we talked to him about it." Frowning, he moved toward the bed. "What do you think is the matter?"

"I don't know. He just said to be *very* careful. And I got the idea from that that he was worried."

George shrugged. "No, I don't think so. He would have mentioned it to us."

"Dear," Mary said to her daughter, forcing cheerfulness again, "shall we tell Bob that it's all right for him to visit you? Are you sure you're up to it?"

Ginny nodded. "Just tell him that I'm still very weak."

"Maybe he should come alone then. He mentioned that some other of your friends—"

"No, that's all right," Ginny said. "They can all come. Just so they realize that I'm not . . . you know, well."

"I'll tell him that."

"I think we ought to talk to that doctor again before we start having a mob up here," George said. "If Ginny isn't feeling well, and if there's something. . . ." He let the thought die. "Let's go round him up—Kildare, I mean," he said to Mary. "I want to talk to him about this."

Mary dropped the comb into her purse and snapped it

shut. "That's a good idea. He's awfully young to be a doctor. Not that he isn't probably competent, but he *is* young." She arose and smiled at Ginny. "We'll be back this evening, dear. You take care."

"Yes, Mother."

"Keep 'em flying!" George grinned.

"Good-bye, Father."

The Dugans headed for the door. Mary paused and waved before going out.

"Good-bye," Ginny said again.

When the door closed, Ginny sighed unhappily. Again, slowly, she lifted the arm and looked at the bandage. Tears began to roll down her cheeks.

Then the door opened again and Miss Walker wheeled another cart into the room. "Soft-boiled eggs," she announced brightly.

Ginny lowered her arm. She glared at the nurse. "I wanted mush."

Miss Walker looked at her wide-eyed. "Darling, nobody, but nobody, ever wants mush."

"*I* want mush."

Miss Walker's eyes narrowed. "Why didn't you say so?"

"You didn't give me a chance. You just decided that I wanted eggs and rushed out of here."

"I don't seem to remember it that way," Miss Walker said, turning the cart around and wheeling it toward the door. "But, if you want mush, lady, it's mush you'll get."

The door closed again.

This time Ginny broke into sobs.

It was midafternoon when Dr. Kildare reappeared in Ginny's room. "You're recovering much too quickly," he said pleasantly.

She looked at him warily. "What does that mean?"

"From the reports I've been getting, it seems that you've entered the cranky stage. That's always a sign that the patient is recovering and wants to get home. Miss Walker tells me that there's been some trouble about the food."

"She's a snitch."

"She's a very good nurse. Why wouldn't you eat lunch?"

"I didn't like what she brought me. First, this morning, she got my order all mixed up. And then at noon she didn't even ask me, she just brought me liver. I don't like liver."

Kildare shrugged. "Well, we don't force-feed around

here. If you don't like what we serve, we won't make you eat it. But we don't make up special meals, either. Not for perfectly healthy patients."

"Healthy?" Ginny said indignantly. "Is that what I am? I'm so weak, I can practically hardly move."

Kildare smiled. "Maybe that's because you don't eat."

Ginny fell silent, pouting.

"Your parents stopped by to see me after they left you," Kildare said. "They're a little concerned. Somehow they got the idea that there's some trouble with your hand. I told them that the stiffness is natural, that it will pass. But I'm not sure that they were convinced." He grinned. "Your mother kept looking at me as if she wanted to spank me."

Ginny faced away from him. "She thinks you're too young."

"Oh." He leaned on the end of the bed. "Have you tried using your fingers again?"

"They just won't work." Her voice was suddenly thick. "I tried, but nothing happens."

"You don't intend to stop trying, though, do you?"

She looked at him, frowning. "Of course not. What do you mean?"

"Just a question." He smiled.

She turned away again. "Dr. Kildare, did you ever make a mistake?"

For a second, he didn't answer. Then he said, "Yes, I've made mistakes."

"It seems to me that all of you people here think you're perfect. Miss Walker and you. I say a thing—I told her I didn't order soft-boiled eggs for breakfast this morning— I say a thing and you make it seem as if I'm trying to make life hard for you. I mean, when you operated on my arm, maybe you did do it perfect. I don't know. All I know is that my fingers won't work. I know, you say it's just stiffness and it will go away. All right. You're probably right. But I can't move my fingers, that's all I know."

Kildare straightened and looked at her uneasily.

"If you say you're perfect, well, I guess you are. How should I know; I'm not a doctor."

"Let's give it a little more time, Ginny. Tomorrow, we'll try the fingers again. And if you still can't manipulate them, we'll . . . well, we'll look into it. But don't worry. There was nothing complicated about the operation. There's no danger."

"Did you ever do an operation like it before?"

"No, but I've studied and I've seen it done many times."

"Well, I guess seeing is as good as doing, isn't it?"

"Not entirely, but—" He studied her a moment, then glanced at his watch. "I have to be going now. I have my rounds to make. You rest. We'll talk about this again tomorrow. If there's a need to do so. It is my guess that by tomorrow the stiffness will start diminishing and that the problem will disappear with it."

"Well, you should know. You're the doctor."

Kildare nodded and turned and moved toward the door.

"Doctor," Ginny said, "some of my friends want to visit me. Is that all right?"

He halted, smiling. "Of course. In fact, it's a good idea. You could do with some cheering up."

"At least, they care what happens to me," Ginny said.

Kildare made no further comment.

5   Visitors

Dr. Kildare returned to Ginny's room that evening while
her parents were visiting. With George and Mary Dugan
looking on, he again asked Ginny to try to open and close
her hand. She raised the arm and seemed to be exerting
an effort to move the fingers—but without success.

Kildare took the hand and gently, one by one, curled
the fingers until the tips touched the palm.

"That's not the same as her doing it," George commented.

"I'm aware of that," Kildare said. He faced the Dugans. "Tomorrow I'll start her on some finger exercises."

"If she can't move her fingers, how can she do exercises?"

"There's no reason why she can't move her fingers," Kildare said. "I think she's a little afraid of the stiffness, but that will pass."

"I'm not afraid," Ginny said.

"She isn't afraid," George said, frowning.

For a second, Kildare had a trapped look. Then he said grimly, "We'll see," and departed.

The next morning he arrived at Ginny's room as Miss Walker was serving her breakfast. He was tossing a small rubber ball into the air and catching it. "For you," he said to Ginny, smiling. "I have a game for you to play to occupy your time."

She looked at him uninterestedly and said nothing.

Kildare turned her hand so that it was palm up and placed the ball in it. "Every time you have a spare moment today, I want you to try squeezing that."

The ball rolled off her hand and bounced on the floor. Kildare chased after it and picked it up and returned to her bedside. "Evidently, I was getting ahead of the game," he said, still smiling. He placed the ball on the small metal stand beside the bed. Then to Miss Walker he said, "Will you try her on this every once in a while today, please? Put it in her hand and let her try to get a grip on it."

"Yes, Doctor."

"Don't hurry it. Two or three times a day will do fine. Let's go at it gradually."

Miss Walker nodded.

"Are you feeling stronger today?" Kildare said, turning to Ginny.

"I don't feel as weak."

"Good. Tomorrow we'll put you in a wheelchair. There's no reason for you to lie around in bed. And then the next day you can try walking. And the day after that—if things are going well—we'll talk about sending you home."

"What about my fingers?"

"What about them?"

"Are you going to send me home if I still can't use them?"

Kildare was silent for a second, then he said, "We'll face that problem when—and if—we get to it. In the meantime, try a little harder."

Ginny looked at him levelly. "Does it make you feel better to think that I'm not trying, Doctor?"

Kildare looked at Miss Walker, who looked away, then back at Ginny. He said no more. He turned and left the room.

Ginny's friends arrived in the late afternoon, after classes. Miss Walker brought them to the room, then withdrew. Bob Carmody was leading the delegation. With him were Ellen Morley, Milly Freedburg, Joanne Hamilton, and Oliver Carpenter. Bob was grinning from ear to ear.

"I'm glad you think it's funny," Ginny said resentfully.

The grin faded. "I'm just glad to see you looking so good," Bob said.

"You do," Milly agreed. "You look great, Ginny. We thought you'd be all sort of washed-out and blah. You know. But you look great. Just like always."

Oliver Carpenter poked his chest with a thumb. "I'm the one who ought to be in here." He touched a finger to a bandage on his cheek. "War wound. Let me tell you about it. I was leading this scouting mission across the enemy lines. There was me, Captain Carpenter, handsome, clean-cut, and also idealistic. Then there was this little guy from Brooklyn, and Hiram, right off the farm from Iowa—sort of innocent—and Aces, a blackjack dealer from Las Vegas. Aces was the cynic, naturally. In other words, typical American boys."

Milly groaned in mock desperation.

"Anyway," Oliver went on, "there we were, pinned down in this shell hole. Bombs bursting in air, rockets' red glare, all that jazz. But we were calm. Hiram was writing a letter home to his Caterpillar tractor. Aces was cheating at solitaire. The little guy from Brooklyn was doing his impression of Red Buttons doing an impression of a little guy from Brooklyn pinned down in a shell hole. Suddenly, one of us went berserk. It was me. 'Let me out, let me out!' I screamed. 'My daddy didn't send me to Yale ultimately to become cannon fodder.' Not surprisingly, it was Aces who saved the day. Underneath he was a softie. He flipped a card at me and"—Oliver touched the Band-aid again— "it caught me right here. The blow brought me back to my senses and I led my men over the top and captured the whole enemy army. I was magnificent!"

Everyone laughed except Ginny.

"The truth is," Bob said, grinning again, "when that glass hit him and he saw a little blood, he almost had kittens."

"The real truth is that I was observing the phenomenon with scientific detachment," Oliver said. "Was it my fault that you and Mr. Allison panicked and did something constructive?"

"You'd think Oliver was really the one who got hurt," Ginny said peevishly. "If you wanted to talk about *his* little scratch, I don't know why you came here to do it. I couldn't care less."

Oliver moaned with pretended anguish. "Get me a chair, someone. I'm growing weak. Everything seems to be getting dark."

"Enough," Milly said to him crossly. She bent over and looked at Ginny's bandage. "That's neat. Almost as good as the Red Cross could do."

"I just wish the doctor could operate as well as he can wrap a bandage," Ginny said. "I guess you know about my hand."

"Sure," Bob said. "Your mother told me that you won't be able to be in the contest. But Ellen's pitching in, so we still have a chance."

Ginny looked piercingly at Ellen.

"I'm going to try, anyway," Ellen said, smiling self-consciously. "I've started practicing more, and I'm really trying now. Not that I'll win, of course, but—"

"Hey," Bob broke in, "where's the old confidence? Why won't you win? Sure you'll win. You won't have Ginny to beat—just those fumble-thumbs from upstate. You're practically in. Have you got a mantel? Start dusting it off for that trophy."

"That's right," Milly said. "Confidence is half the battle. Positive thinking. That's why Ginny always won; she believed in herself."

"There was a little more to it than that," Ginny said sharply. "And more to it than just practice, too."

"The question is," Oliver said, "if Ellen loses, will education retrogress to the stone-age level?"

The others ignored him.

Bob took Ellen playfully by the shoulders, and, holding her at arm's length, stared her sternly in the eyes. "I am Abdul ben Ali, your friendly neighborhood hypnotist. You are under my power. Repeat after me. 'I will win. I will win. I am invincible.'"

Ellen giggled and said, "I hear you, master. You will win. You are invincible."

Bob threw up his hands. "How can an artist work under these conditions—with an empty mind?"

Ginny had observed this horseplay between Bob and Ellen with increasing irritation. Now she said acidly, "All that is *very* funny. But it isn't going to help keep the championship. And neither is practice nor positive thinking."

"What the girl is trying to tell us," Oliver grinned, "is that she's talented."

"I didn't mean that," Ginny snapped.

Oliver leaned forward, grinning teasingly. "Listen, tell us about your operation. Did you get pictures? Could we—dare we be so bold as to ask—could we see your scar?"

Ginny glared at him.

"Oliver, turn to another channel, will you?" Joanne said. "Ginny isn't feeling funny. Why should she? What's fun about being in a hospital?"

"Getting out," Oliver replied.

"Ginny, maybe you could give Ellen some tips on technique," Bob said, trying to ease the growing tension.

"I don't see why I should," Ginny said. "All she has to

do is practice. That's what everybody seems to think. That's all there is to it—just practice."

Bob shrugged. "Okay. Just an idea."

"It might help," Ellen said to Ginny. "I need something. My mother says I can do it. And the kids say I can do it. But *I* don't say so. I get jittery just thinking about the contest. Practice is one thing, but being out there in front of all those people—and the judges—that's something else."

"Just keep practicing," Ginny said tightly. "I'm sure you'll do fine. And keeping the championship isn't important, anyway. Ask Oliver; he'll tell you."

"Maybe we better go," Milly said.

Oliver put on his silly grin again. "Go? Now? Just when the action is getting nasty? Let's don't go, let's sell tickets."

Milly put her hands on his shoulders and turned him around and headed him toward the door and pushed. "Go." Then she trailed after him. "We'll come back in a day or so if you're still here," she said back to Ginny. "Get well." Then she and Oliver disappeared out the door.

"See you," Joanne said, and she hurried after them.

"Don't let Oliver bother you," Bob said to Ginny. "You know Oliver."

"Sure, he doesn't mean anything," Ellen said. "It's just his way. He has a complex."

"He can keep it away from me," Ginny said shortly.

Bob spread his hands. "He's just kidding. Don't have kittens about it."

"Don't you know anything else to say?" Ginny flared. "Anytime anybody does anything, you always say they're having kittens. Do you *always* have to say that? What kind of a vocabulary is that? Kittens! Kittens! Everything's kittens!"

Bob pulled in his head sheepishily. "Sorry. It's just an expression."

"It sure is!"

Ellen backed toward the door. "Well . . . see you." She looked at Bob. "I'll wait outside."

"Okay."

The door closed behind Ellen.

"What's eating you?" Bob said to Ginny.

"You better go," Ginny said. "She might not wait."

"I want to know what's eating you."

"Are you going to start *that* now? If it isn't 'kittens,' it's 'what's eating me.' Boy!"

"Okay," Bob said resignedly. "I guess you're tired or something."

"That's right, I'm tired. Good-bye."

"I'll be back tomorrow."

"Don't force yourself. Don't you have to go to Ellen's and cheer her on? She's going to be the next champion, isn't she?"

"What are you talking about? I've never been to Ellen's house in all my life."

"Then how do you know she has a mantel?"

"What? A mantel? A— Oh, you mean what I said about dusting off the mantel for the trophy? That's just an—" He waved a hand disgustedly. "Skip it."

"She's waiting," Ginny said, tears coming to her eyes. "You better hurry."

"I'm going." He strode across the room, went out, and closed the door noisily behind him.

Ginny choked back the tears. She wasn't going to cry about it. Let them all desert her; she wasn't going to cry.

About a half hour after Ginny's friends had gone, Miss Walker came back into the room. Ginny was listless, staring vacantly into space. She didn't look up.

"Nothing like visitors to cheer up the patients," Miss Walker said amusedly.

Ginny peered at her blankly.

Miss Walker carried a chair from the windows to the bedside and sat down. She picked up the rubber ball from the metal stand. "Remember?"

Ginny nodded.

"Hold out your hand."

"I don't think I can."

Miss Walker took hold of Ginny's hand and turned it over and placed the ball in the palm. "Now then, try to close."

Ginny shook her head. "I can't. I explained that to Dr. Kildare. I can't. If I can't, I can't."

"I said 'try' to close. You're not trying."

"I am."

Miss Walker returned the ball to the stand. "Let's see what we can do about the stiffness," she said, and she began to massage Ginny's fingers. "I suppose you're anxious to get back to school," she said, speaking gently. "Your friends seemed nice. Who was that tall boy with the red hair and the gorgeous blue eyes?" She smiled at Ginny.

"Bob Carmody."

"He was looking scary all the way up to the room. Then when we got to the door he suddenly blossomed out in a big grin. Apparently he didn't want you to know that he was worried."

Ginny said nothing.

"Redheads are supposed to have a temper," Miss Walker said. "Does he?"

"Not much. Except sometimes."

"How do your fingers feel now?"

"Cold."

"Ummmm . . . poor blood circulation. Well, a little more massaging."

Ginny sighed deeply.

"The next time your friends come, you might tell them that there's a Coke machine on the next floor down. And maybe I could get you some snacks from the kitchen."

"I don't think they'll be coming back."

"Oh, I imagine they will. Or did something happen?"

"Nothing special."

"Then I'm sure they'll be back. If you know beforehand, let me know, and I'll use my influence with the kitchen." She placed Ginny's arm on the bed again, with the hand palm up, and said, "Now, again."

"If you want to."

Miss Walker put the ball in Ginny's hand. "Use your will, too. Not just your fingers. The mind controls muscle action, you know. The muscles don't work independently, they react to the message from the brain."

"That's interesting," Ginny said indifferently.

Miss Walker waited. Nothing happened. "Well?"

"I can't."

The nurse's patience faltered, her eyes narrowed, she started to speak harshly—then she caught herself. "All right," she said quietly, "we'll try again later." She took the ball from Ginny's hand and put it back on the stand. Then she got up and returned the chair to the windows. "There's nothing physically wrong with your hand, Ginny," she said, heading for the door. "A little more time and it will be as good as ever before."

"How do you know?"

Miss Walker paused. "I know."

"It must be nice to be so sure. Dr. Kildare is sure, too.

Everyone is sure but me. But who am I? I'm only the one who can't use my hand. What do I know about it?"

Miss Walker studied Ginny concernedly for a second, then she went on out the door.

6   A Call for Help

The next day, as promised, Dr. Kildare delivered a wheelchair to Ginny's room.

"The speed limit for this room is forty-five miles per hour," he said. "And the penalty for breaking it is mush every morning for breakfast."

She smiled weakly.

"Tomorrow," he went on, "we'll fit you out with a sling for your arm and you can try getting around on your own—walking, in other words."

"A sling?"

"Only to protect the wound—to remind you that it's there and keep you from bumping it and breaking open the stitches."

"Oh."

Dr. Kildare and Miss Walker lifted Ginny from the bed and put her in the wheelchair. When she was settled in the seat, Kildare said, "You can operate it with your other hand. Or, you can try it with your right hand if you want to."

"I don't plan to go anywhere."

"Not even to the windows?"

"Well. . . ." She looked up at him. "Will you wheel me, please?"

"You do it."

She lowered her eyes. "Never mind."

Kildare gave in. He wheeled her to the windows and positioned the chair so that she could look out across the courtyard.

"That's spring out there," he said. "Remember spring? Balmy breezes, green trees, a tangy odor in the air."

"I haven't been here *that* long," Ginny said crossly.

"Tomorrow, when you're on your own feet again, I'll take you for a stroll in our courtyard."

"Fine," she said. But she said it without enthusiasm.

Two days later, Ginny was still spending the daytime hours in the wheelchair. Kildare had tried to get her to walk, but she protested that she was too weak.

Kildare did not press. But, that afternoon, after visiting hours, he had a talk with her parents. He told them that he thought it would be best for Ginny to remain in the hospital for a few more days. "The progress is slower than we expected," he explained.

George Dugan looked at him sourly. "What progress is that? She's out of bed, that's about all I can see. What about her hand? You said it would be stiff for a couple of days, then it would be all right. She can't move it. Is that what you call 'all right,' Doctor?" There was a pinkness in his cheeks that indicated that he was having trouble holding onto his temper.

"I was wrong," Kildare said. "I based what I told you on our previous experience, but, obviously, Ginny's case is not following the normal pattern. However, there is no reason—no reason that is apparent—why she shouldn't begin responding to treatment. We're using physical therapy—"

"That rubber ball," George said curtly. "Is that what you mean?"

"That and heat and massages and . . . well, as I said, there's no reason why she shouldn't begin responding."

"You were wrong before, Doctor," Mary said.

"Yes, I was."

"You know," George said, "she's just another patient to you, but to us, she's our daughter. We don't want anybody fooling around who doesn't know what he's doing."

"You're free to call in another doctor."

George hunched his shoulders. "Well, I guess there's no need for that yet. But let's have some action. If we don't, we'll have to do something. I don't know what, but something. Another doctor or something."

"She's so depressed," Mary said.

Kildare nodded. "She certainly is. It puzzles me."

"Who wouldn't be?" George asked. "If I couldn't use my hand, I'd be depressed, too."

"But the depression set in before there was even a hint of trouble with her hand," Kildare said. "It started that first day, right after you and your wife visited her the first time."

"Is that supposed to mean something?" George asked defensively. "Are we supposed to be a bad influence on her or something, is that what you're trying to say?"

"Of course not." Kildare smiled. "I was simply trying to establish the beginning of the depression in time."

"Okay. Just so we're clear on what's what." He got to his feet and his wife arose, too. "We'll just let things ride for a few more days, I guess. But let's see some action, eh? I don't want to have to go over anybody's head on this."

Kildare's smile held steady. "That's kind of you."

"Well, I like to get along with people—if they'll let me. You're probably doing your best." He took his wife's arm. "But let's see some action," he said. Then he steered Mary toward the elevators.

The rest of that day and that evening were restless for Kildare. He could not get his mind off Ginny. He was certain that there was no physical reason for her inability to regain the use of her hand, but he had no alternative reason to explain it. After a time he found himself doubting the certainty that there could be no physical cause for the disability.

When Kildare finished his tour of duty that night, he stopped in at Wilson Everleigh's room in the residency. Everleigh was in bed, still recovering from the virus that had struck him down in the operating room the day that Ginny had been brought into Emergency.

"How long can you keep up this faking?" Kildare grinned.

Everleigh was reading a book. He put it down. "I have a year and two months to go on my residency; I figure I can carry this through till then. How are all my patients?"

"I'm sorry to be the one to tell you this, but they're getting well without you."

"Ingrates," Everleigh grumbled. Then he brightened. "Say, how's that kid who needed the blood coming along— the one I passed out on?"

"She has me worried," Kildare said.

"For real?"

Kildare nodded. He explained that Ginny was still un-

able to use her hand, then said, "Is it possible that I did something wrong?"

"It's possible," Everleigh said. "Of course it's possible. What exactly did you do?"

Kildare outlined each step he had taken after Everleigh had turned the operation over to him. When he finished, Everleigh said, "It sounds right. That's exactly what I would have done."

"Then why can't she use that hand?"

"I said, 'It sounds right.' I wasn't there, I don't know that you did everything you say you did. Not that I'm doubting your word, Jim. But I don't *know*. It's possible that you think you did everything you say you did, but that . . . well, it wouldn't be the first time a mistake was made."

Kildare shook his head. "I'm sure."

"There's another possibility," Everleigh said. "Maybe there's an 'unknown' in this."

"What do you mean?"

"An unknown element. Maybe something happened that you weren't aware of. We had a case like that a few months ago. A woman had a cancer operation. Afterward, she had severe pains in her left arm. No one could explain it. There was no known reason for the pain. The surgeons thought it was an emotional reaction."

"Psychological?"

"That's what they thought. They tried psychiatry; they tried hypnosis. But nothing worked; she kept insisting that she had the pains. Then one of the surgeons had a wild idea and they checked it out, and that was it. They found that the nerves in her arm had been scarred by the radiation. Completely unexpected. See what I mean? The unknown element."

"There wasn't any radiation involved in this," Kildare said.

"So? Maybe it's some other unknown. I'm not saying that it is—but it's possible."

Kildare sighed heavily.

"I'd take it to Dr. Gillespie if I were you," Everleigh said.

"Yes, I think I had better." Kildare got up, scowling darkly, and moved toward the door.

"Thanks for stopping in to cheer me up," Everleigh said gloomily.

The first thing the next morning, Kildare telephoned Dr. Gillespie's office and asked for an appointment. His secretary allotted Kildare a half hour at noon. And when Kildare arrived, at twelve o'clock exactly, he found the Medical Director eating his lunch at his desk.

Dr. Gillespie was a tall, trim man with graying hair and an aggressive, bulldog jaw. His expression did not often soften. His responsibilities were countless and he was acutely aware of each and every one of them.

"Pretend you don't see this," he said to Kildare, indicating the lunch on the tray on his desk. "As a doctor, I'm unalterably opposed to the modern practice of grabbing a quick lunch on the run." He bit into a roll. "What's on your mind?"

"I could come back later," Kildare said.

"In other words, it's something that, if you had the choice, you'd prefer not to discuss with me."

Kildare colored slightly. "You're busy."

"No, I'm not. I eat lunch at my desk like this to project an image. I want the trustees to think that I'm unexpendable." He gestured impatiently. "Come on, what is it?"

Kildare sat in the chair across the desk from Gillespie.

As the Medical Director ate, Kildare told him what had occurred from the moment that Ginny had been brought to the hospital to the present time. The story and the meal ended at approximately the same time.

Gillespie sat back and touched his lips with a napkin, then tossed the napkin onto the tray. He looked squarely at Kildare. "I'm compelled to express the same thought that Dr. Everleigh did," he said. "That is, the possibility that you committed an error. I suspect that you, too, are giving that possibility some consideration."

"I don't really believe it, though," Kildare said. "Since last night, I've been through that operation a hundred times —in my mind. And I'm positive that I did everything that was necessary."

"If there's absolutely no doubt in your mind, why are you here?"

"Well. . . ."

Gillespie shook his head. "No, you're not as sure of yourself as you would like to think you are." He smiled fleetingly. "And that's good. When a doctor begins to consider himself infallible, he loses a good deal of his worth."

Kildare straightened in the chair. "Where do we go

from here? I frankly don't know."

"Let's have a talk with your patient," Gillespie said, arising. "At this point, I'm working too much from speculation. When we raise the possibility that you committed an error, we must also consider the alternative—that you didn't. So, first, let's look elsewhere for the cause of the trouble." He headed for the door.

"What about the 'unknown' that Dr. Everleigh mentioned?" Kildare said, following him.

"Let's exhaust the 'knowns' first. Until we do that, the 'unknown' doesn't actually exist, does it?"

They left Gillespie's office and went to Ginny's room. When they entered, Ginny was finishing her lunch. She was in the wheelchair at the windows with an apparatus that held a tray attached to the arms of the chair. She was using her left hand to eat. Miss Walker was standing by.

Kildare introduced Dr. Gillespie. Then Gillespie apologized for interrupting during the lunch hour.

"I'm through eating, anyway," Ginny said. "The food doesn't taste very good—kindy of woody."

Miss Walker took the tray from the chair and departed.

"I suppose you'll be glad to get back to your mother's

home cooking," Gillespie said to Ginny, leaning back against the windowsill.

"I would be," Ginny said. "Except—"

"Yes, Dr. Kildare has told me about the problem." Gillespie glanced momentarily toward Kildare, who had seated himself on the edge of the bed. "I doubt that it's permanent, however. The solution exists, it's simply a matter of finding it—wouldn't you say?"

Ginny shrugged.

"You have marvelous control over your emotions for a girl your age."

"I don't think I have anything much to be happy about," Ginny said. "How would you feel, Dr. Gillespie, if you knew you weren't ever going to be able to use your hand again?"

"Is that the way you feel? You have no hope at all?"

"Well, nothing is happening. I just sit here, and every once in a while Miss Walker puts that rubber ball on my hand and it rolls off. I can't get much hope from that, can I?"

Gillespie did not answer. He went to Ginny and bent over and looked closely at the bandage. "Scissors, please," he said to Kildare, not looking up.

Kildare went to the cart that was standing near the end of the bed and got a pair of surgical scissors and brought them to Gillespie, then watched while the Medical Director snipped off the bandage and inspected the wound.

"Healing nicely," Gillespie said.

"How can you tell what's wrong on the inside by looking at the outside?" Ginny said.

"You know that something is wrong on the inside, do you?"

She looked away. "It just makes sense. I can't use my hand, and it's not because the skin is too tight, so it must be something inside. It makes sense."

Gillespie returned to the window.

Kildare wheeled the cart to Ginny's chair and began applying medication in preparation for re-bandaging the wound. "Do you still feel the coldness in your fingers?" he asked.

"Sometimes. Sometimes not."

"Now, as I understand it," Gillespie said, "when you try to manipulate your fingers you get absolutely no reaction. Is that correct?"

Ginny nodded her head woodenly.

"No reaction whatsoever?"

She lowered her eyes. "Well, maybe there's some sort of a feeling. I'm not sure."

"Not sure? This is important to you, isn't it? It must be, considering your obvious state of depression. Yet you say you're not sure."

"What I mean is, yes, there is a kind of feeling. But that doesn't change the fact that I can't use my fingers, does it?"

Gillespie shook his head. "No, it doesn't." He turned to the window and looked out onto the courtyard. "How are your grades in school, Ginny?"

She looked up, caught off-guard by the question. Then she smiled faintly. "They're good, Doctor. I have a B-plus average. Are you going to psychoanalyze me?"

He turned back to her, smiling. "Am I that obvious?"

"Well, if I were a doctor and I didn't know what was wrong with a patient, I might think it was something in the patient's mind. That would be the easy way."

Gillespie smiled amusedly. "I can believe that you have a B-plus average," he said. Then, to Kildare, he said, "Ready there?"

Kildare had completed the bandaging. He nodded and wheeled the cart away.

"Good-bye, Miss Dugan," Gillespie said to Ginny, still smiling. "The meeting has been a pleasure, and enlightening—and perhaps even helpful. I hope I'll see you again."

"I'll be right here," she said, looking at him evenly.

The two doctors left the room and walked down the corridor a few steps, then halted.

"Youngsters today are much too bright," Gillespie said. "When I was that age and I was told something, I accepted it without question."

Kildare laughed. "That, I doubt."

"Well, I pretended to, anyway. That was the rule: A boy didn't question his elders. But, I suspect that the new way is the better way. Questions lead to knowledge."

"Unless they're a means of evasion."

"True. But in this case we're going to have to assume they're not. Let's take a look inside, where Ginny is so sure that the something wrong is hiding. X-rays. Examine the tissues, see how that muscle is healing. But—" he began walking again, and Kildare accompanied him, "—but keep another thought in mind. I got the impression that the girl wants to stay here at Blair."

"I can't agree," Kildare said. "She doesn't like anything about the hospital. She doesn't like the food, she's irritable with the nurses—and with me."

"Let me put it another way, then. I suspect that there's somewhere else that she doesn't want to be. Or, in still other words, that the hospital, disagreeable as it is to her, is less disagreeable than the other place—wherever that other place may be."

"Is that why you asked her about her grades?"

"Yes. It occurred to me that she might be running away from some unpleasantness at school. But apparently not." He halted again. "You mentioned that the depression started just after her parents visited her on that first day. Is there a connection?"

Kildare thought a moment, then said, "There may be. The family situation seems pleasant enough, normal enough. But then, I haven't spent much time with them when they were all together. It's worth looking into."

They began walking again.

"There's one thing I ought to mention," Gillespie said. "Sometimes when we're looking for an answer, we look harder in the place where we *want* it to be than where it's most likely to be."

"Would you translate that?"

"It would be better for you—for your ego—to find the answer in Ginny's family situation than in your own error."

It was a second before Kildare replied. Then he said only, "The theory is undoubtedly true. I'll keep it in mind."

Gillespie nodded. "Do that."

7   A Special Visitor

The next morning, Kildare requested that X-rays be taken of Ginny's wound. She was scheduled for later in the day, and when the time came, Kildare accompanied her as she was wheeled to X-ray by Miss Walker. When the technicians took over, he and Miss Walker walked back toward the ward together.

"I don't suppose there's any point in asking if there's been any progress with the rubber ball," Kildare said.

"No progress, Doctor."

"Are you puzzled by this, Miss Walker?"

"Of course," she said. "But, maybe they'll find the answer in X-ray."

"I doubt it." He remained silent for a few minutes, then he said, "Do you have the impression that she isn't really trying to recover the use of her hand?"

"I thought that at first," the nurse replied. "I wanted to give her a good spanking. But now—lately—I'm not so sure. She does seem to be trying. Unless she's a better actress than most sixteen-year-olds. I could be wrong, though."

"Has she ever said anything that gave you the idea that there's something on the outside—outside the hospital, I mean—that frightens her? A person or a situation?"

"No. She's disappointed; there was some kind of a baton-twirling contest she was going to compete in and now she can't. But I don't see why that would frighten her."

"Her parents mentioned that. Her mother especially. She was quite upset about it, in fact. But I didn't pay too much attention to it at the time. It didn't seem important."

"It still doesn't," Miss Walker said.

"No, I suppose not. Still, you never know. What seems unimportant to us might be a matter of considerable consequence to her."

"Maybe. But if I were looking for a reason for her inability to use her hand, I think I would put more trust in the X-rays than in the idea that she was upset about missing out on a baton-twirling contest."

"Yes, but when the X-rays show that there's nothing wrong, where do I go from there?"

Miss Walker smiled. "Is the fix in, Doctor?"

"Pardon?"

"You seem so sure that the X-rays will show that there's nothing wrong."

Kildare laughed. "My hope seems to be running a few lengths in front of my head, doesn't it? You're right. I'd better wait for the X-rays before I blame this on baton twirling."

It was clear that Miss Walker agreed.

It was late afternoon when Ginny was returned to her room from X-ray. The nurse who brought her back placed her chair near the windows. After the nurse had gone,

Ginny sat staring bleakly out into the sunny green warmth of the courtyard. She watched the doctors and nurses passing from one building to another, listened to the occasional bursts of laughter that floated up to her windows. Every few minutes, she sighed wistfully.

The X-ray technician had told her—she hadn't asked, but he had told her anyway—that the X-ray photos would be ready for Dr. Kildare's inspection the next morning. She wondered if the result would end this—this waiting for the doctors to realize that her problem was physical, not emotional. She doubted it. They would never admit that they were wrong. In the morning, Dr. Kildare would come to her room and say, "Well, Ginny, the X-rays prove it— your trouble is all in your mind." And that would be that.

But she could be as stubborn as they were. She knew that the trouble was physical, and she would not budge an inch from the hospital until they admitted it, too.

The door opened and Miss Walker came into the room. "Are you up to having a visitor, Ginny?" she asked.

"Who?"

Miss Walker smiled. "The tall, blue-eyed redhead. He came while you were in X-ray. I told him he could wait."

"Is he alone?" Ginny eyed the nurse warily.

"Yes."

"All right then."

Miss Walker departed. A few minutes later, the door opened again and Bob entered the room. As before, his smile was large and warm. "Hi."

"Hi," Ginny answered coolly.

He moved to the windows and stood facing her. "I see you're still here."

"Brilliant."

"I mean, we all thought you'd be out by now. Your mother said you'd be coming home in a few days, and that was almost a week ago. What's the holdup?"

"Nothing. Just that I expect that I'll be a cripple for life, that's all."

Bob grinned. "Aw, come on."

"That happens to be the truth. I can't use my hand anymore. Something happened. And they can't find out what."

Bob sobered. "Actually?"

"Did you come here to call me a liar?" she asked curtly. "If you did, you can go. You've said it, so you can go."

Bob hiked himself up onto the windowsill. "I didn't call

you a liar. It just seems funny, that's all. You got a little cut on your arm and all of a sudden you can't use your whole hand. I don't doubt it, if you say so, but it seems funny."

"I guess it does to you, a big expert on cuts and arms and medicine and everything. But it isn't very funny to me. You don't see me laughing, do you?"

"I didn't mean funny funny, I meant strange funny. Can't they do anything?"

"They're not even trying. They're just saying it's not true. But they'll find out." A sudden urgency had come into her voice, as if she were pleading desperately below her bravado for Bob to believe her—and now, tears came to her eyes. "They'll find out," she said again. And she looked down at her hands, the one gripped into a small fist, the other hanging limply from the end of the sling.

Sympathy welled up in Bob. He searched his mind for the right thing to say. But before he found it, the pressure of his own silence caused him to speak prematurely, and he said the wrong thing. "Maybe you're just imagining."

Ginny lowered her head and the tears rolled freely down her cheeks. She tried to hold back the sobs, but they were stronger than her will. Her shoulders shook.

Bob squirmed uncomfortably on his perch on the window-sill. "What I meant was, maybe it's not as bad as you think. If they can do something, I know they will. Doctors don't go around not doing anything when there's something they can do. Do you see what I mean? Have a little —I don't know—hope."

Ginny choked back the sobs. But she did not raise her eyes.

Bob smiled feebly. "Everybody said to say hello. Milly and Joanne and Mary and Marge. Mr. Allison, too. And Ellen. Say, listen," he said, with a sudden enthusiasm, "she's doing okay. Ellen, I mean. She's shaping up. That positive-thinking business is working. She's really beginning to believe that she might come out on top in the contest." He laughed. "Maybe she will. Marge says it's not just in her mind. She says she's really getting the hang of it."

Ginny lifted her eyes and looked at him wrathfully.

But Bob, unaware of the reaction, went on. "It's probably psychological. She knows she doesn't have to compete with you so she figures that now she actually has a chance to win. That can do wonders. And she has this cheering section.

Every afternoon after school, Marge and Milly and Joanne, the whole bunch of them, go to Ellen's house and give her that old *rah rah* while she practices. You know, like they used to do with you."

"They don't have time to come here to see me," Ginny said tightly, "but they can go there. That's just fine. I appreciate that."

Bob frowned. "They came here."

"Once."

"Once was enough. They got the idea that you didn't want them around. I got the same idea."

"You're here."

He shrugged. "Maybe I'm a glutton for punishment."

"And maybe you're feeling guilty. It seems awfully funny to me that suddenly nobody wants to have anything to do with me. Why is it? It isn't me. I'm still the same me."

"What are you getting so excited about? What do you mean, nobody wants to have anything to do with you? Are you cracking up or something? What do you expect? They came here and you almost bit their heads off. They just figure that you're cranky, being here in the hospital, and they'll give you a chance to get over it."

"Oh, sure. So, in the meantime, they all go to Ellen's house. You, too, I suppose. I suppose you're there every afternoon with all the rest of them. I guess you're in the cheering section, too."

"It so happens that I'm not. But only because I don't happen to be *rah rah*. What's the matter with it? They want her to win."

"Well, she *won't* win!"

"I don't know about that."

"*I* know. It takes more than practice and it takes more than a cheering section."

"You said that the last time. I get the idea."

"And when she doesn't win, we'll see how long she has a cheering section. We'll just see."

"So . . . we'll see."

"It won't be—"

Ginny was interrupted by the sound of the door opening. Her mother entered the room.

Mary Dugan looked slightly flustered. "I'm late today," she said apologetically. "Hello there, Bob. Isn't this nice?"

Bob hopped down from the windowsill and stood smiling. "Hi," he said.

"Your father couldn't come today," Mary said to Ginny. "Something at the office. A truck broke down somewhere in Ohio and it had a shipment that was due in Chicago yesterday, and. . . . I don't know. Anyway, he'll be here this evening. How are you, Bob? Ginny's father said that you stopped by and that he told you that Ginny was still here."

"I'm fine," Bob said. He looked at Ginny. "Well, maybe I better be going."

"No, don't rush off," Mary said. She sat down in one of the chairs and put her purse in her lap and began removing her gloves. "You're such good company for Ginny. She's always telling me what good company you are." She smiled at Ginny. "Aren't you, dear?"

"No," Ginny said belligerently.

Mary studied her for a second, frowning. Then her smile broke through again. "I was just thinking, on my way to the hospital, how *won*derful it must be to be the age that you children are. You don't appreciate it, of course. You take it for granted. But, believe me, it's a marvelous time of life. No cares, no worries. All you have to do is have fun. I was thinking, Ginny and Bob have the whole summer

ahead of them. They can be together and just *enjoy* them- selves. Isn't that *won*derful?"

"Mother, if you don't mind—"

Mary laughed. "You children take everything so serious- ly. Even having fun. 'Youth is wasted on the young.' Some- one said that. And it's certainly true."

"Well . . ." Bob said weakly. He moved a step closer to the exit.

"Have you and Ginny made any plans yet for the sum- mer?" Mary said to him. "Ginny never tells me a thing about what you two have in mind."

Bob looked uncomfortable. "As a matter of fact," he said, looking at Ginny, "it's kind of up in the air—the summer, I mean." He was reflecting on the fact that he had decided to buy his brother's Ford and that there would not be any money available during the summer for entertaining Ginny. He did not want to discuss the matter with Ginny in the presence of her mother, however. "I have a plan that might —uh, well, what I mean is, it's too early to say. It's still spring and summer is a good distance away. If you see what I mean."

"Oh," Mary said disappointedly.

"Good-bye, Bob," Ginny said coldly.

"Yeah, I guess I better be going." He nodded to Mary. "Good-bye, Mrs. Dugan." Then to Ginny, he said, "I'll see you."

She did not reply.

Bob hesitated another second, then departed.

"Ginny, that wasn't very nice of you," Mary scolded. "What's the matter? I've never seen you act like that toward Bob before. Bob is a wonderful boy. I like him very much."

Ginny remained silent.

"I know that look." Mary sighed. "You're blaming me for something. I don't know what *I* did. I simply asked if you and Bob had any plans for the summer."

"We haven't ever had any plans, any summer," Ginny said. "We just do things. We don't sit down at the end of spring and make up a schedule for the summer. And, as for this summer, I don't think there will be anything."

"For heaven's sake, why not?"

"Isn't that pretty obvious? Bob isn't interested anymore. You heard him. He has something else in mind. And it includes Ellen Morley, if you want my opinion. The whole time he was here he talked about practically nothing else but Ellen. It's pretty obvious, isn't it?"

Mary fluttered her fingers nervously. "Well, you'll have to do something. You're a much prettier girl than Ellen. I don't believe it. I don't believe that Bob would. . . . Well, I just don't believe it. He's too sensible."

"What does sensible have to do with it?" Ginny snapped.

"Here now, don't you talk that way to me," Mary said. "It's not my fault that—" She softened. "I'm sorry, dear. Probably I did say the wrong thing when Bob was here. But I didn't do it intentionally." She tangled her fingers together tightly. "You'll have to apologize to Bob, that's all. He'll understand."

Ginny looked at her perplexedly. "Apologize to him for what?"

"I don't know. You must have done something to make him lose interest in you."

"I did something, all right. I stood in front of a window when a baseball went through it. Is that what I'm supposed to apologize for?"

"It must be more than that, dear. That doesn't make sense."

"Ellen is going to win the contest," Ginny said. "That

makes sense, doesn't it?"

Mary laughed. "Little Ellen? Of course she isn't."

"She isn't 'Little Ellen.' She's the same age that I am. And she *is* going to win the contest. She's been practicing —and hard. And everyone says she can win. Milly thinks so and Marge thinks so and Joanne thinks so—and Bob thinks so."

"Well, *I* don't think so."

"Have you been watching her practice?"

"Darling, if I've said it once, I've said it a thousand times. It isn't practice that counts the most, it's talent. Haven't I told you that? And *you* have talent."

Ginny looked down at her hand. "This is what I have."

Mary caught her breath. "Don't say that. I won't listen to it. The doctor said that your hand will be all right after a while, and it will. Don't ever even *think* anything different. I forbid it."

"Mother," Ginny said pleadingly, "I'm sixteen. You can't order me to think this or not to think that."

Mary sighed sorrowfully. "I know. I'm sorry. But this is all more than I expected, and it's got me so upset. But, believe me, dear, your hand will be all right. The doctor is very sure everything will be fine."

"Then I have nothing to worry about," Ginny said dismally.

"Of course not. But don't say it that way. Believe it."

"I'll try."

"Good." Mary smiled. "And don't fret about Bob, either. I'm sure that you'll be seeing just as much of him this summer as you did last summer. He's such a handsome boy. And you're so pretty. And Ellen is. . . . Well, Ellen is a nice girl. I like her very much, but she doesn't have your talent. And talent is very important. You'll see. This is temporary. Ellen may have him now, but next year you'll be champion again. Then you'll see."

Ginny was silent for a second. "I don't think I would want it that way," she said.

"You must learn to compromise, dear," Mary said. "Life is a compromise, one compromise after another." She toyed with her gloves. "Someone said that. I don't recall exactly who." She bit her lips. "Maybe it was me."

8   One Reason Down

Kildare had been on duty the next morning for no more than ten minutes when he received the call from X-ray. The nurse told him that the plate was ready for him to view. When he reached the lab, Joe Ellison, the chief technician, had already placed it on the screen.

"I thought you might be in a hurry," Ellison said.

Kildare laughed. "Is the word out that I have myself a dilemma?"

"There's talk." Ellison smiled. He was a heavy-bodied, ruddy-complexioned, blond man, with a smile that exposed a superfluity of gold. He pointed to the screen. "And there's your proof," he said.

Kildare looked closely at the image on the screen. He smiled and sighed relievedly. The picture showed that the skeletal muscle was healing perfectly.

"It couldn't be clearer," Ellison said.

Kildare went to the desk, picked up the phone, and called Dr. Gillespie's office. When Gillespie came on, Kildare said, "I have the X-ray on Ginny Dugan. Will you come down and look at it? I'll keep it on the screen."

"What does it show?"

"Perfect."

"There's no reason for me to come down. You've never given me any cause to doubt your word, Doctor."

"I want someone to back me up."

"I repeat: Your word is sufficient."

The phone went dead.

Kildare hung up, then said to Ellison, "Keep that on the screen."

"For how long? I need the viewer."

"Just another couple minutes."

Kildare went out into the corridor. He saw a resident, Dr. Willart, coming toward him. "Will you come in here a second, Doctor?" he asked. "I need a witness."

Willart grinned. "Who's the lucky girl?"

"Not that," Kildare said, taking Willart's arm and steering him into X-ray. "You see, a little over a week ago a patient was brought into Emergency when I was on duty and—"

"I know the story," Willart broke in. "What do you want me to witness?"

Kildare pointed to the screen. "Right there. Is that muscle healing correctly or isn't it?"

Willart studied the image. "It is. Is that your stitching? Pretty neat—for an intern."

"Okay. Then you're my witness." He turned to Ellison. "And, Joe, hang on to that plate. Don't let it get lost."

"Have I ever lost a plate?" Ellison said indignantly.

Kildare and Willart left X-ray together. Walking down the corridor toward the elevators, Willart said, "Now that you're in the clear, does that settle it?"

Kildare's exultation faded. "Not quite," he said. "The

fact is, all I've done is eliminate one possibility. The problem still exists."

"But it's not your problem any longer," Willart said. "You did what was expected of you, and you did it correctly. So you're out of it."

Kildare looked at him sideways.

"You're right," Willart said. "It's still your problem."

When the Dugans arrived at the hospital that afternoon to visit their daughter, Kildare was waiting for them in the corridor. He stopped them before they reached her room.

"There's been a new development," he said. "I'd like to discuss it with you."

"About time," George said.

"Yesterday," Kildare said, "I had X-rays taken of the wound area. There was a chance that I had committed an error when I performed the surgery. But the X-ray showed that the muscle is healing as expected."

George frowned. "Who said it wasn't?"

"No one actually said it, but there was some speculation. I believe that you had the idea that Ginny's trouble might be a result of something I did wrong."

Mary spoke up. "Doctor, what does this mean now—now that you've taken the X-rays?"

"It means that there is no physical cause to keep Ginny from using her hand."

"You say she's faking, is that it?" George queried.

Kildare hesitated. "Well. . . ."

"Is that what you're saying, or isn't it? If there's no physical reason, she must be faking—right?"

"Not—"

But George Dugan was already on his way down the corridor toward his daughter's room. "We'll see if she's faking."

Mary Dugan and Kildare hurried after him. They caught up to him just as he entered Ginny's room.

"Mr. Dugan—" Kildare protested.

But George ignored him. He stomped across the room to where Ginny was seated in the wheelchair. "Where's that ball—that rubber ball?" he demanded, stopping in front of her.

Ginny stared at him, startled.

"Where is it?"

"On the stand," she murmured.

He looked across the room toward the metal stand that was beside the bed, saw the ball, then went for it. When he returned to the wheelchair, he held the ball out in front of Ginny. "You see this? You're going to take it in your hand and you're going to squeeze it. You can do it. Don't tell me you can't. We know now."

Ginny only continued to stare.

"They took X-rays," George said. "I guess you know about that. They found out there's nothing wrong with you. You're fine. Understand? So you take this ball."

She shook her head. "Father, I—"

"Don't give me any argument." He took her hand and held it out and placed the ball in the palm. "We've had enough of this nonsense! Now, you squeeze that ball. Squeeze it!"

Tears came to Ginny's eyes. "Father, I can't. I can't."

"Do it!"

"I can't."

Angrily, he closed her fingers on the ball and held them closed. "You can do it. Those fingers work. Now you do it by yourself. You do it, Ginny, or I'll— You do it, that's all. You do it! I know you can!"

"Father, please, please," she sobbed. "I can't. I want to but I can't."

"You're going to squeeze that ball if I have to—"

Kildare suddenly stepped forward and took the ball from Ginny's hand. "Enough!" he said sharply to George Dugan.

"Listen, Doctor, you're the one who—"

"I'm *not* the one," Kildare broke in on him. "I didn't tell you to come in here and browbeat her like that."

"I know how to handle my own daughter."

"Mr. Dugan, you don't even know how to handle yourself. Temper isn't going to get you anything but high blood pressure." He headed for the door. "Come with me."

Mary tagged after him.

George held his ground for a second. Then he sighed heavily and looked at Ginny, who was still crying. "I'm sorry, honey," he said. "I guess you know what you can do and what you can't do. I'm sorry."

"I can't," she wept. "Father, I just can't."

"Okay, okay. I know. I believe you. I'm sorry." He patted her gently on the shoulder, then followed Kildare and his wife to the door of the room.

In the corridor, George said, "I guess I owe everybody an apology."

"Not me," Kildare said. "I didn't want to say it, but the truth is, I thought the same thing that you did—that she was faking. But, after this, I no longer believe it. For some reason, she is actually unable to use that hand."

"Then find the reason," George said, becoming combative again.

"We'll try."

"Try? What kind of a place is this? What do you mean, you'll try? That's my daughter in there. What do you expect her to do, go through life with her hand that way?"

Mary began to weep.

"Stop it!" George snapped.

The command only started the tears flowing more heavily.

"She'll be a cripple," Mary sobbed. "What will happen to her? I wanted her to marry a nice boy. But she won't—"

"Mary!"

"Mrs. Dugan," Kildare said soothingly, "you're letting your imagination run wild. In the first place, if it does turn out that her hand is permanently impaired, that doesn't mean that her life will be ruined. There are people with far greater handicaps than Ginny's who lead normal lives. In the second place, I can't believe that we won't find the solution to the problem. It may even be that it will work itself out in time. We'll continue the therapy, and, in the meantime, we'll investigate the other possibilities."

"Like what?" George said.

"For one thing, there may be a psychological cause."

"Rubbish!"

"Mr. Dugan, how can *you* be so certain when we're not certain? It isn't inconceivable that the affliction has a psychological basis. It isn't even improbable."

"I say rubbish. I happen to know my daughter. She's no more insane than I am."

"Did I mention insanity? There are degrees of psychological disturbance. Your quick temper, in fact, is a degree. But I haven't implied that you're insane."

George snorted. "Maybe the way you're avoiding the main issue is a degree, too, Doctor. The point is, before Ginny was hurt, her hand worked fine. Now it doesn't. She's been here over a week and all I can see is that she's worse off than when she came in. And I want something done. I don't want a lot of gobbledygook about psychology, I want action. And if I don't *get* action, I'm going to take steps."

"Would you like to talk to the Medical Director?"

"What for? He's a doctor, too, isn't he? All you doctors stick together. I don't want any more talk from anybody. I want action."

"We're going to do everything we can, Mr. Dugan."

"Maybe that's not enough."

"You're free to remove your daughter from this hospital any time you want to."

"And maybe I will; maybe I'll do just that."

Kildare lifted his hands in resignation. "What more can I say?"

"You've got a responsibility, don't forget that," George said. "Don't try to weasel out of your responsibility. That hand was all right before. It's your job to fix it."

"I just told you; we'll do everything we can."

"All right. Okay. Just don't try to weasel out." He turned to his wife. "Let's go, Mary. We'll have to talk about this. We'll have to decide what to do."

She nodded, blinking away tears.

The Dugans moved away toward the elevators. Kildare watched them for a second, then returned to Ginny's room. She had stopped crying. She was staring dejectedly out the window.

"I think the fireworks are over for a while," Kildare said, smiling sympathetically.

"Please, don't mind my father, Dr. Kildare. He's that way. It's the way he gets things done. Maybe it's necessary sometimes, but he isn't that way all the time—not even often. He's a very good father."

"I don't mind," Kildare said. "Sometimes when people don't understand a thing, they react to it with anger. And I don't blame him for not understanding this. I don't understand it either. All we can do is keep looking for the answer."

"Then you do believe me?"

"I believe that you're truly unable to use your hand. It's the cause that eludes me. As your father mentioned, the X-ray showed that the muscle is healing."

"Until you find out, you'll keep me here, though, won't you? You won't send me home."

"We'll keep you here for the time being. Tomorrow we'll begin a series of examinations. Since we're not sure what we're looking for, we'll have to look everywhere—and thoroughly. It will take time."

"It's not that I don't want to go home," Ginny said. "It's just that I don't want to go home this way. It would be a mistake. Here in the hospital is where we have the best chance of finding out what's wrong with my hand."

Kildare smiled noncommittally. "We'll talk about it later. Right now I'd better start setting up those tests. We'll want to get at it bright and early in the morning." He headed for the door. "Incidentally, I'm going to have an easy chair brought in here. I don't think you need that wheelchair any longer."

"But why go to all that trouble? This is comfortable."

He halted at the door. "No trouble. And you might as well start walking again. Then you can get around without having to have a nurse wheel you. Our nurses have enough to do—and there aren't enough of them to do all the things that must be done. It would be a help to us."

"Well, if that's what you want," she said, pouting slightly. "I'll do whatever you say."

"Good girl." Kildare smiled at her.

From Ginny's room, Kildare went to the charge desk. He checked the roster of residents and interns to find out where Dr. Everleigh was assigned, discovered that he was in Emergency, then went there. Everleigh was in the small office outside the operating room. He was slouched in one of the chairs with his feet up on the desk.

"Slow day," Everleigh explained. "A sudden quiet has settled on the world. Do you suppose this is the lasting peace they're always talking about?"

Kildare laughed. "Do you?"

"Hopeth springeth eternaleth."

Kildare dropped down into the chair that faced him. "Do you remember the other day when we were talking about an 'unknown'? I may have a situation like that right now."

"The girl?" Everleigh said, lowering his feet to the floor and straightening in the chair.

"The girl." Kildare nodded. "I checked out the surgery and it was right on the button. The muscle is healing, it looks fine. But still she can't move her fingers. There's the possibility, of course, of a psychological intrusion, but I can't settle for that and send her away without looking elsewhere for the cause. Do you have any suggestions?"

"Schedule her for every examination we're equipped to give—and hope."

"That's what I'd planned to do. You mentioned that other case, and I thought it might suggest something."

Everleigh shook his head. "I don't see any connection. That was a cancer case where radiation was used. The only similarity is that there was an unexplainable aftereffect— unexplainable until it was found, of course." He suddenly cocked an ear. "The peace is ended."

Kildare listened and heard the distant sound of an ambulance siren. He got to his feet. "Wish me luck."

"Luck," Everleigh said, rising. "And keep out of drafts." He hurried toward the operating room, on his way to scrub up.

9   Nobody Understands

The examinations began the next day. Kildare explained to Ginny's parents why the tests were necessary and told them it would be preferable for her to remain in the hospital while they were being made. George agreed truculently and Mary wept. Nevertheless, the decision was made, and a tutor was engaged to come to the hospital every day to keep Ginny current with her schoolwork.

At first Ginny went to the examinations resentfully.

But her scratchy temper seemed to be caused more by her wheelchair being taken away from her than by the various discomforts of the examinations. As the days passed, however, her attitude gradually changed. Her spirits lifted. She no longer kept entirely to her room but began to visit the other wards, to make friends with other patients, and to chat with the nurses on duty whenever they had a spare moment.

Her favorites among the patients were a Mr. Grosvenor and a Mr. Morris, who had beds side by side in one of the wards on the second floor. Morris and Grosvenor were both in their sixties. Grosvenor was frail and quite pale. Morris had the look of a tufted sparrow; he was small and chubby and bald except for two feathery wisps of white hair above his ears.

Ginny did not ask the men what kept them in the hospital; she felt that asking that question would have been prying, and that if they wanted her to know they would tell her. She assumed, though, that their disabilities were not very serious, for both men were as spirited and impish as children.

Grosvenor and Morris passed a considerable amount of

their time playing checkers. The board was on the metal stand between their beds, and they would lie on their sides and reach out to move the playing pieces. Their games were far from orthodox. They argued over each move, their attentions wandered to happenings going on around them in the ward, and they battled over which one had won the most games. Ginny became a sort of referee.

She would walk into the ward in time to hear Grosvenor say, "Move your red there in the second row, Morris, or I'll have a double jump. You're like a child. If I didn't tell you where to move, I'd be ahead of you a thousand games instead of a hundred-and-eighty."

"Aha!" Morris would snort disgustedly. "Don't think I don't see your strategy. If I move my red and escape the clutches of your double jump, that'll set you up for a triple jump. And it's not you that's ahead of me a hundred-and-eighty, it's me that's ahead of you. And the number is two-hundred and forty-six, not a hundred-and-eighty. Hsst! Look, the nurse is bringing Mr. Watson a piece of mail. Brown envelope. That means it's from his daughter in Pittsburgh."

"Might be from the Light Company. They also use

brown envelopes. Maybe he didn't pay his electric bill. They're suing him. Play your red, will you?"

Morris would scowl. "I don't choose to. I choose to cogitate. And why would Watson be getting his electric bill here in the hospital? I say that letter's from his daughter in Pittsburgh. She works for the Government and the Government's got brown envelopes like that, too."

"The truth is, she don't live in Pittsburgh, she lives in Detroit. Ginny, where does Mr. Watson's daughter live? It's Detroit. I remember it specifically because Watson told me himself that he drives a 1949 Ford. That's association. Didn't he say that, Ginny?"

"He did say that he drives a Ford." Ginny usually found it safer not to take sides. "I don't remember the year."

"There you are, Morris. She lives in Detroit. Ginny heard it the same as I did. Right from Watson's own lips. Now, I suppose you're going to tell me that Watson doesn't know where his own daughter lives."

"Detroit it may be. But you're wrong about her working for the Light Company." Morris would move a checker. "There!"

"Now you've done it. You make a move like that and

I'll take the game from you. I can finish you off in six more plays; it's all in my mind, crystal clear. You want to take it back and move that red in the second row like I told you to, Morris?"

"I do not."

"That's an illegal move you made. I leave it up to Ginny. Ginny, is that an illegal move or isn't it?"

"I don't know much about checkers."

"What's illegal about it?" Morris's tufts of hair stood straight up. "Nothing. You got yourself a double jump there, Grosvenor. Take it. You got to take your jumps; that's the rule."

"Oho! What about my option? I've got the option. You got the first move in the game, so that means that I've got the option. I get one chance to break the rules—that's the option. I leave it up to Ginny."

"I don't think I've ever heard of an option like that." Occasionally she was forced to take sides.

"And neither has anybody else, except maybe Watson's daughter in Pittsburgh."

"Fair!" Grosvenor was never defeated. "Fair, that's all I want to be. If there's some kind of doubt in your minds about my option, I'll accept a compromise. I'll give up all claim to my option if Morris will take back his last move. And it's Detroit. Detroit, not Pittsburgh, Morris."

"We've had no confirmation on that. Watson driving a Ford car doesn't prove where his daughter lives. The only Government office I know of, outside of Washington, D.C., the capital, is in Pittsburgh."

"Now there's a piece of intelligence for you! Why, they've got Government offices in every city of the universe. What branch of the Government is she with?"

"It's not the 1949 Ford automobile department, I'll tell you that. Take your jump, Grosvenor."

And so it usually went.

But there were other times, times when the two men had no zeal for checkers and were strangely subdued. At such times, although their good humor remained, the friendly baiting of each other ceased, and they were quietly reflective.

One day when Ginny visited them and they were in this mood, Grosvenor said to her, "Why don't you go out into the sunshine, girl? This is a dark place in here. No matter how many fancy lights they put in, it's still a dark place and always will be. Go out where the sun is."

"Do you want to be alone?" she said, slightly hurt.

"Alone? Nobody wants to be alone, not even a hermit. You know why a hermit goes off to a cave? So somebody'll come and visit. It's not that I'm trying to chase you away that I said that about the sun. It's for you. There's little enough time in life as it is to get out into the sun."

"True enough," said Morris. "All the important and necessary things that have to be done, they have to be done in the dark places. All the figures that have to be figured up, and all the calculating that has to be done before there are any figures to be figured up. If I had it in my power, I'd do something about the situation. When you get to be of an age, you appreciate the sunshine."

"I'm not sure what you mean," Ginny said.

"Sure not. You're not of an age. When I was young, I didn't notice the sunshine much either."

"If I was to sum up, I'd say that that was a pretty good picture of myself, too, when I was young," said Grosvenor. "All the important things I did in the dark places, looking back, I don't know that they were as important as I thought they were at the time."

"Things have to be done," Ginny said. "That's what

makes things move, and makes things better for everyone."

Grosvenor nodded. "Things have to be done, all right. But maybe not in such a scramble-bamble hurry. Maybe with a little more grace and gentility. We're like that fellow that drove his car from New York to Los Angeles in some-thing-something hours. Broke all the records. And he was talking about it to this other fellow, and this other fellow says, 'I've driven that trip myself and it's a beautiful ride. What did you think of the mountains in Pennsylvania, and the lake in Chicago, and the prairies in Kansas, and the Grand Canyon, and the desert? What did you think of them?' he says. 'Didn't see them,' says the other man. 'Had my eye on the speedometer all the way.' "

"That's the way it is," Morris said. "We start out young and we race ourselves to get to be of an age and we miss all the sights along the way." He looked toward the windows. "That's a lovely lot of sunshine out there."

Ginny felt somewhat pressured, as if they were attacking her personally. "I don't mean to be disrespectful," she said, "but isn't it possible that if you were still young, you'd feel differently? I mean, wouldn't you do things, lead your lives, the same way you did them before? It's all very well to look back and say that the important things weren't really important. But they were important at the time, weren't they? What I mean is—"

"It's very clear what you mean," Grosvenor said. "And maybe you're right. Now, here I am, of an age, and I can look back and remember an instance when I felt driven to do a certain thing. Driven like that fellow drove from New York to California. It was more important to me than life itself—so I said, anyway, though the fact is that nobody put it up to me that I had to make the choice. But I can understand what you mean. At the time, I didn't want to hear any gibble-gabble from any old man about 'easy does it.' I knew what was important and nobody was going to tell me different."

"Did you do it—this thing?" Ginny asked.

"Yes."

"Did it make you happy? Would it have changed your life if you hadn't done it?"

"Well, girl, I can only guess about that. But I would say . . . yes. Yes, I think it changed my life. A couple years after I'd done it, I saw the mistake it was. I didn't make the mistake again. So I guess it can be said that it changed my life. As for happy—well—I guess—"

"But suppose this important thing would change your life for the worse if you didn't do it? Do you understand? What I mean is, right now there is something that is very important to me. But I can't do it because—well, just because. And not being able to do it, it's going to change my life in a bad way."

"How sure are you of that?" Morris asked.

"Positive."

"I think we need a for-instance," Grosvenor said.

"On the contrary," said Morris. "This is a matter for philosophy. And a philosophy fits every instance or it's not much of a philosophy, is it?"

"A for-instance would facilitate the process of conjecture," Grosvenor said.

"Grosvenor, you're nosy. We don't need any details, all we need is a general picture." He turned again to Ginny. "What's this horrible thing that's going to happen in your life?"

"From now on, people are going to think differently about me," she said. "The way they thought about me before, I had a chance of someday having all the things

I want in life—the things that are important to me. But now, because of—well, because of their not looking up to me as they did before—because of that, I'm going to miss so much. And I worked for it. I don't know, maybe I'm not being clear. Can you understand what it is to be popular, and then to be—ordinary?"

"That's about the most—" Grosvenor began tartly.

"Let's not chop the onions before we get the peels off," Morris broke in, scowling at his friend. "I can still remember the day when I was of the opinion that what the rest of the world thought of me was important."

"You *should* remember," Grosvenor said. "It was only yesterday."

"Grosvenor, are we going to develop a philosophy for this child that can carry her safely through the storms of life or are we going to bicker like two children over the last piece of candy on the dish?"

Grosvenor shrugged. "Develop. Go on, develop. But to develop you got to have a basic material. Here is a girl who thinks because she's not Miss Popular, everything she's going to get in life is going to be second-best."

"Think, Grosvenor. Isn't it possible that that's true? Not

for you. Not for me. Not for ninety-nine out of a hundred people. But for Ginny maybe it's true. It depends on what she wants and how bad she wants it. Am I right? Grosvenor, am I right?"

Grudgingly, his friend made a face of agreement.

"If she wants a limousine—if having a limousine automobile is the most important thing to her—and she gets Mr. Watson's old car instead, then for her what she gets is second-best."

"I don't care for your analogy," Grosvenor said. "Make it a limousine and a bright red convertible—this year's."

"It shall be done."

"That isn't what I want," Ginny protested. "I don't want anything as special as that. I just want—well. . . ." Her wants suddenly seemed impossible to explain.

"You want the best," Morris said for her. "It's understandable. Who doesn't? The question is, how bad do you want the best? For some people it's the best or nothing. It's like food and drink to them; if they don't get it, they die."

"No!" Ginny flared. "You're making me sound silly. I don't want anything more than the everyday things, what everyone else has. But to get them, you have to be special—a little special, anyway."

"This will be a surprise to all the ordinary, everyday people who have all the ordinary things," Grosvenor said. "And I say that as probably the most ordinary of all the ordinary people."

"Again, you're too fast with the onions," Morris said. "What the child means is that she wants the ordinary things to be given to her. She wants them as a gift. She's right. For this, she must be special. Ordinarily, the ordinary people work for the ordinary things they get. Only the special people receive them as tribute."

"You don't understand!" Ginny snapped. "You *won't* understand. I did work. I told you that. I worked hard. I practiced. I practiced for hours and hours and hours. And now everything that I worked for has been taken away from me. What am I supposed to do? Make creaky jokes? It *is* important to me! I have all my life ahead of me, and what I want is—" She suddenly broke into tears. "What I want is—"

"Girl," Grosvenor said softly, "we understand. It's just that we're looking at it from a greater distance than you are—it doesn't seem so big to us. But it's not because we don't understand. Now—"

But Ginny whipped around and ran, crying, out the door.

Grosvenor turned to Morris and sighed and said, "She won't be back."

"She'll be back. She loves us. We're cranky old men and everybody loves cranky old men."

"You said the wrong thing to her," Grosvenor said.

"Sometimes the wrong thing is the right thing." Morris sighed, as Grosvenor had sighed—sadly. Then, "Ring for the nurse to bring the checkerboard, old man," he said. "Maybe there's time for one more game."

After that day, Ginny stopped going to the ward where Grosvenor and Morris were patients. At the same time, her spirits fell again. The up and down baffled Kildare, for there had been no change in the condition of her hand to cause the rise and fall.

About two weeks after the tests were begun, though, an incident occurred that gave him a clue to her baffling behavior. It was in the afternoon and Kildare was on his way to Ginny's room when he met her mother in the elevator. Mary Dugan was carrying a baton and an overnight bag.

"I have her costumes in here," Mary said, indicating the bag. "I thought that if she had her baton and her costumes they might inspire her. Twirling was very important to her."

"Yes, you told me that."

"I'm ready to try almost anything," Mary said. "This is so terrible. You don't know, Doctor, what it is to be a girl and to have something like this happen. George doesn't realize either. But, for a girl, it's just . . . horrible."

"And you think that seeing the baton and the costumes will help?"

"She might try harder," Mary said.

The elevator door opened and they stepped out and walked together down the corridor toward Ginny's room.

"Mrs. Dugan," Kildare said, "you think this is psychological, too, don't you?"

"Of course not," she denied quickly. "It's just that I'm willing to try anything."

"But if—"

"I'm not going to argue about it with you, Doctor. I want

to help my daughter, that's all. I don't think anything—that it's one thing or another. I just want to help."

"All right, Mrs. Dugan."

They reached the room and Kildare opened the door and held it open for Mary to pass; then he followed her in. Ginny was in the easy chair that Kildare had provided for her. There was a book in her lap. She looked up and smiled as Kildare and her mother entered. Then she saw the baton, and a sudden look of fright came into her eyes.

If Mary Dugan saw the fear, she gave no sign of it. She steamed on into the room, suddenly bursting with cheerfulness.

"Darling, you look wonderful today!" She beamed. "Absolutely wonderful! Doesn't she, Doctor? Well, time certainly is a healer. I've always said that."

"Hello, Mother," Ginny said. Her voice was small and she seemed to be drawing away.

"Surprise, sweetie. Look what I've brought you." Mary held out the baton. "And this isn't all." She put the baton and then the overnight bag down on the bed. "Close your eyes—no peeking," she bubbled. Then she unsnapped the bag and opened the lid. "Ready?" Out came a brief blue and gold costume. "Surprise!"

There was no peeking because Ginny had not closed her eyes. The costume was no surprise to Ginny—and neither was it a pleasure. She looked, and she forced an infinitesimal smile, but the look in her eyes, again, was a look of alarm.

"I thought you'd be pleased," Mary said, hurt by Ginny's lack of enthusiasm.

"I am, Mother. Thank you. But, why don't you. . . ." She looked quickly around the room. "You could put them in the closet over there. I won't really be needing them for a while."

Mary chewed her lips, then said, "I could put the costumes away. But the baton, wouldn't you like to have it out, so you could try to. . . ." She gestured vaguely with a limp hand. "Well, you know."

Ginny lowered her eyes. "You better put it away, too. I won't have any use for it."

"I thought it would be inspirational."

Ginny looked at her sharply. "Mother, I don't want it!"

Kildare interceded. "It would probably be best to put them in the closet," he said to Mary. "If Ginny wants them, she'll know where they are."

Mary looked at him, again biting her lips; then she closed the bag, and carrying it and the baton, moved toward the closet.

"I stopped by to change your dressing," Kildare said to Ginny. "But I'll come back later."

"You can do it now." Clearly, she wanted him to stay.

"No, later." Kildare smiled. Then he went out.

When he reached the charge desk, Kildare asked the nurse on duty to call him when Mrs. Dugan left Ginny's room. He returned to the routine of making his rounds.

The call came about forty-five minutes later, and Kildare immediately went back to Ginny's room. She was still in the chair, but she was no longer reading; the book was closed on her lap. Her eyes were moist and Kildare suspected that she had been on the brink of crying when he entered the room. He picked up the book and took it to the metal stand, then got a chair and the medical cart and sat down to change the dressing on Ginny's wound.

With the scissors, he cut the bandage. "Did your mother take them back with her?" he asked.

"No, they're in the closet."

"Your mother told me before how important baton twirling is to you, but I guess it didn't sink in—until today. Why does it mean so much?"

She spoke in her small voice again. "It isn't important. I do it . . . I did it, rather . . . just to fill time, to have something to do. That's all."

He removed the bandage and dropped it into the waste container. "I don't know much about it," he said. "I suppose it takes a lot of practice."

"If you want to be good, it does."

He began applying the medication. "You're some sort of a champion, I understand."

"State. I was, anyway. I won't be long. The contest is next Saturday, and after that I won't be champion any more."

"Your parents must be very proud of you. A B-plus student and a champion."

"I suppose so."

"All that practice probably cuts down on your other activities, but it's undoubtedly worth it to be a champion. Or is it?"

"Of course it is. For a girl, anyway. But you wouldn't

understand that. My father doesn't, either. He thinks it's nonsense. If I've heard him say that once, I've heard him say it a million times—that it's nonsense."

"I think I understand," Kildare said. "Girls thrive on attention, and being a champion generates attention. That's not difficult to understand."

"That's not it at all." Ginny frowned. "It's not just the attention."

Kildare began re-bandaging the wound. "What is it then?"

"I told you, you wouldn't understand. You're not a girl."

Kildare laughed. "You could try me. Go ahead, enlarge my knowledge of the female of the species. Tell me."

Ginny was silent for a minute, observing him speculatively as he worked with the gauze. Then she said, "Well, with boys it's different. For them, just being a boy is enough. I mean, they're sort of masters just because they're boys. I know all about this emancipation of women and all that, but having the vote and equal opportunity and that, that doesn't change the nature of things, does it? My mother, for instance. Being able to vote doesn't change the fact that my father is boss. Do you see?"

"You were going to tell me about girls."

"That's the point. A girl has to do something special. If she doesn't, she gets passed up."

"It seems to me that I've met a good number of married women who can't do one single thing that's particularly special."

"Sure. But who are they married to?"

"Some quite pleasant chaps."

"I'll bet."

"What does your mother do that's so special?"

Ginny frowned again. "That's different. She's already married, but I'm only sixteen. It will be years before I'm married."

Kildare looked at her puzzledly. "I'm not sure I understand the connection between my question and your answer."

"Of course you don't—you're not a girl."

Having replaced the bandage, Kildare got up and wheeled the cart back to its corner. Then he returned and sat down again, tipping back in the chair and rocking gently. "You must have started out practicing baton twirling when you were very young," he said. "I'm sure you didn't become a champion overnight."

"Not so long," she said. "Only a couple of years. I have a sort of talent for it. But before that it was violin, and before that piano. I didn't do as well at them. My mother was disappointed."

"Did she suggest the baton twirling?"

Ginny thought for a moment. "I don't remember. Maybe she did. Or maybe I did. But she approved. Especially after I . . . well, got good at it. I wish I could say the same for my father. He thinks it's silly." She looked closely at Kildare. "What do you think?"

"I don't see anything especially silly about it," he said. "But, on the other hand, it isn't a sport that sets my blood racing, either. My opinion isn't particularly important, though, is it? What counts is what you think. Where do you stand? On your mother's side, or your father's side, or in between?"

"Well, you see, my father doesn't understand."

"That wasn't the question."

"I don't know how else to answer. To my mother it's important, and to my father it's silly."

"Don't you have an opinion of your own?"

"Yes, I guess I do—in a way. I'm a girl, like my mother is a woman, and I understand that it *is* important. Maybe I'm not as sure about *why* as she is. But, she's a woman and I'm a girl, and she should know, shouldn't she?"

"Perhaps so." Kildare smiled. He got to his feet and walked slowly toward the windows. "You say the contest is Saturday. Are you going?"

"How can I? I'm here."

"We're not keeping you prisoner. You visit the other patients, you go to the examining rooms. I think we could manage to give you a day off."

"But isn't it really much more important that I stay here and have the examinations? The sooner you find out what's wrong, the sooner I'll be able to go home for good."

Kildare did not commit himself on the question. He reached the windows and stood with his back to Ginny, saying nothing for a moment. Then he faced her again. "I haven't seen your friends here for quite a while."

She shrugged. "They have other things to do. Why come to a hospital and be bored stiff? I don't blame them."

"Still, you'd like to see them again, wouldn't you?"

"I guess so."

"The contest would be an opportunity. They'll all be there, I imagine."

"Oh, they'll be there, all right," she said tartly. "The whole crowd. All gushy over Ellen Morley. She's the girl who's—" Ginny suddenly silenced herself and looked at Kildare belligerently. "What are you trying to do? Why are you asking me all these questions?"

"Because I'm interested. You're my patient."

"Then do something to help me," she said, her manner softening a bit. "Don't waste your time asking me a lot of questions about things that don't matter."

Kildare smiled. "All right, Ginny. No more questions." He walked toward the door.

"Dr. Kildare, I really don't care about that contest. If you think I do, you're wrong."

"Of course you don't," he said amiably, reaching the door.

"I don't. I *don't!*"

But the effort was wasted; he was gone.

From Ginny's room, Kildare went to the charge desk. He made a telephone call to the Dugan home and talked to

Mary Dugan. He asked that she and her husband meet him in the main reception area that evening when they came to visit their daughter. She wanted to know why. He told her that what he had to say was much too complicated to discuss on the phone, and that he wanted George Dugan to be present when he said it. She assured him that she and her husband would keep the appointment.

Kildare, who was off duty by then, was waiting in Reception that evening when the Dugans entered the hospital. He went to them and escorted them to a relatively quiet section of the area. When Mary was seated, she immediately knotted her fingers together. George sat on the edge of the chair, hunched forward, and his chin and the cigar in his mouth jutted forward, too, as if to keep Kildare at a distance.

"You said you wanted to talk," George said.

Kildare smiled. "How do you know I don't have something pleasant to say?"

"I don't know anything, except that Mary said that you called her."

"If you don't know what I'm going to say, why are you sitting there cocked, ready to jump at me?"

George groaned aggravatedly, then settled back in the chair. "Okay. Say. Make your speech and I'll listen."

"I had an enlightening talk with your daughter today," Kildare said. He smiled to himself. "I can't say that it proceeded with the sort of logic I'm accustomed to in talking medicine with doctors, but it was revealing nevertheless."

George smiled thinly. "I know what you mean by that, at least. Sometimes I have a little trouble keeping up with her, too. Now me, when I have a thing to say, I say it. Out with it. No zigging, no zagging. Right on the penny."

Mary spoke up. "Not everything can be said that way. Some things aren't clear-cut. They're complicated."

George laughed. "To hear a female tell it, anyway."

"Your daughter is a female, you know, Mr. Dugan," Kildare said.

"What's that supposed to mean? Is it supposed to be big news?"

"It means that you have no right to expect her to think as you do—always with bright, brilliant, clear logic."

"Look," George said, "I don't need any lessons in how to talk to my daughter."

"How about listening? Do you know how to listen to her, too? Or is the communication between you all one-sided?"

"The fact is," Mary said, "he doesn't listen to anyone."

George ignored the comment. "Doctor, this is family stuff. I don't see that it concerns you. Now, you said you had something to say. Let's hear it."

"What Ginny and I talked about most was baton twirling," Kildare said.

George groaned. *"That* business."

"She gave me the impression," Kildare went on, "that she considers it quite important, but,"—he turned to Mary—"she doesn't quite know why. She thinks she knows. She has a vague idea that her whole future happiness depends on doing something 'special.'"

George leaned forward. "Did she say that?"

"Not in those exact words. But I didn't expect her to. I don't demand pearl-pure reasoning and articulation from a sixteen-year-old. In fact, not even from adults."

"Or, in other words, you're making a wild guess. Not that I don't go along with you. I've said it from the very first; this baton business is nonsense. But, putting words in Ginny's mouth, that's something else. I want some proof, not just a harebrained theory. No offense intended."

"Thank you." Kildare faced Mary again. "The point I'm trying to make is that Ginny's idea is not necessarily her own. From what she said, my guess is that it's yours, and that she is, so to speak, stuck with it."

"I haven't ever forced my ideas on her," Mary said indignantly.

"Not intentionally, perhaps. But she loves you. She loves you both very much. Isn't it possible that she's accepted this idea because she wants to please you? Love is a force —a very strong force; stronger even than physical or intellectual compulsion."

"I don't know," Mary said, weakening. "How can I answer you? But, even if you're right, what's wrong with the idea?"

"Wrong with it? It's based on the belief that standing out in the crowd, being the focus of attention, is the magic key to happiness. For some, that may be true. But not for everyone. Forgive me, Mrs. Dugan, for being personal. But—are you happy?"

Mary drew back, startled. "Of course I am. That is, normally, I'm as happy as anyone."

"Would you say that you're exceptionally popular?"

"No. I wouldn't want a thing like that. I have my friends, and. . . ." Her shoulders fell; suddenly she understood what Kildare was intimating. "But I didn't tell Ginny that the world would end if she weren't popular," she protested.

"Did you imply that she needed that 'magic key'?"

George broke in, speaking to Mary. "He's got you there. The way you stew about grabbing the applause, it's no wonder she thinks she has to sit up on top of the mountain or nobody will see her. The doctor's right. Even me, I'm not so blind that I haven't seen that."

"What have you done about it?" Kildare said to George Dugan.

"I told them," George said. "I told them that this stick-throwing business was nothing but a lot of nonsense. Now, you take me. If I worried about being popular, I'd still be where I was twenty years ago—driving a truck for a living. Getting the job done, that's what counts—and nothing else." He hooked a thumb toward his wife. "You tell her, Doctor."

"That brings us back to this," Kildare said. "Are you really aware that your daughter is a girl? Frankly, I doubt that you are. You expect her to think like you, to reason like you—in fact, to *be* you, a miniature of you. But she isn't."

"Look," George said, half-disgustedly, half-impatiently, "maybe you're a social worker or something, I don't know. But I know this. The trouble with Ginny is not what I want her to be or what Mary wants her to be. It's her hand. That's the sum total of it. And all this talk about who did this and who did that isn't going to change that fact one bit. Now, where do we stand? That's the question. What's the verdict?"

"I think your daughter's physical disability is directly related to what we've been talking about," Kildare said. "If I didn't, I wouldn't have said all this."

George looked at him exasperatedly. "Do you mean to say that because Mary wants her to sit up on top of the heap, and because I don't go for a lot of silly junk, that because of that, she can't use her hand? Is that—is *that* what you're trying to say?"

"Who is Ellen Morley?"

George let out a puff of air. "Now, there's an answer for you. That's *really* an intelligent answer!"

"Ellen is a friend of Ginny's," Mary said.

"What's this Ellen's connection with baton twirling?"

"Some of Ginny's friends think that Ellen will win the contest now that Ginny won't be able to compete. But it isn't true. Ellen is a very nice girl, but she isn't talented."

Kildare turned back to George. "In answer to your question: Yes." He leaned forward. "When I was talking to Ginny today, the one thing that I especially noticed was her reaction to my questions about the contest. I encouraged her to go to it—as a spectator, of course. But she declined. Do you see? Her interest is not so much in baton twirling as in what it has given her—attention, the spotlight. And when the contest ends, someone else will be champion, the spotlight will shift."

"So for weeks she's been pretending that she can't use her hand? I can't buy that, Doctor."

"She isn't pretending," Kildare said. "Her subconscious has taken over and made her believe—and in a sense, it's true—that her hand is crippled. She wants to stay in this hospital. Or, to be more accurate, she doesn't want to return to a situation where she is no longer the center of attention. She is convinced that popularity is all-important."

"And that's what you have to say, eh?"

Kildare nodded. "That's what I have to say."

"Are you a psychiatrist, Doctor, or are you just an intern around here?"

"I'm an intern."

"Not a psychiatrist."

"No."

"I think you're looking for an out. Somewhere along the line, you've bungled the whole thing. You say you took X-rays and they showed that you did a crackerjack job. Well, maybe so. Maybe so. But let me ask you this: Who took those X-rays? Somebody here at the hospital, right? One of your pals, I guess. I said it before: You doctors stick together. I think you're looking for an out. I said it before, and I say it again. You're looking for an out." He got to his feet. "Come on, Mary, we've heard enough."

Mary looked straight at Kildare for a second, and there was an apology in her look. Then she arose.

The Dugans walked away toward the elevators.

Kildare slumped in the chair. He sighed sadly. Then he

searched his own conscience, wondering if George Dugan could be right. Was he looking for an escape from the responsibility?

He could not believe it.

10 Examination

When Dr. Gillespie's secretary arrived at the office the next morning she found a caller waiting for the Medical Director. Dr. Kildare was scooted down in one of the large leather chairs in the anteroom. He was bleary-eyed.

"Were you on duty all night, Doctor?" she asked, seating herself at her desk.

"You might say so." He smiled. "I wasn't officially on duty, but a patient kept me awake almost all night. Will

Dr. Gillespie be in soon, do you think?"

"Any minute now." She got a dustcloth from one of the drawers of her desk, then disappeared into Gillespie's private office.

Kildare closed his eyes—but a second later he was snapped to attention again by the sound of Gillespie's voice.

"Why wasn't I notified that my office had been turned into a hotel?"

Kildare groaned and sat up and stretched. "I didn't get much sleep last night. That's why I'm here. May I have a minute? It's about Ginny Dugan."

"All right. Come on in."

They entered Gillespie's office. The secretary had just finished dusting the top of Gillespie's desk.

"Stirring up the germs again, eh?" Gillespie said to her. "Let them lie. A dormant germ is a happy germ. You irritate them and they go around attacking people."

Laughing, the secretary departed.

Kildare sat down in the chair that faced the desk. Gillespie hung his hat in the closet, then dropped his briefcase beside the desk and settled in the swivel chair. "All right, what is it?"

For the next quarter of an hour, Kildare talked without interruption. He told Gillespie first about his conversation with Ginny, then about the follow-up talk with her parents. When Kildare finished, Gillespie got up from his chair and began to pace the room, saying nothing. Kildare watched and waited.

After a few minutes, Gillespie returned to his desk. "It's an interesting theory you have," he said. "And it's very possible that it's right. There is, however, the equal possibility that it's wrong. You're aware of that, I suppose."

"Naturally."

"Where do you plan to take it from here?"

"I don't know. That's why I've come to you."

"The ideal would be to get her parents to see that they're in part responsible—that it's a reaction to their attitudes. But apparently there isn't much chance of that. Do you agree?"

Kildare nodded.

"That leaves the girl. Somehow, you'll have to make her understand what she's doing to herself."

"I thought you might help me with that."

"Aha! That's why you're here."

Kildare leaned forward. "I don't have a great deal of trouble getting her to talk to me. But listening to me, that's another matter. Now, if I had some gray in my hair. . . ."

"Well, since we don't have a makeup department here in the hospital, I suppose that means that creaky old Dr. Gillespie is elected." He got to his feet. "Shall we? What better way to start the day."

They left Gillespie's office and went to Ginny's room. Miss Walker was just wheeling away the breakfast cart. Ginny was sitting in the easy chair. She eyed Kildare and Gillespie warily as they entered.

"Good breakfast?" Gillespie smiled. "What did you have?"

"I had eggs."

"How do you like our eggs these days?" Gillespie said, going for one of the chairs near the windows.

"Fine."

"That's a change, isn't it? Dr. Kildare tells me that you're much happier with us these days than you were at first. He says that you're making friends. Expecting to settle down here, are you?"

Ginny frowned. "What's the matter with making friends?"

"Nothing," Gillespie said, placing the chair in front of her and sitting down. "But it's odd that you're suddenly so content. Most people spend their hours in a hospital clawing to get out."

"I don't want to make any trouble."

"Ummm-huh."

"What I mean is, I know that you're doing everything you can for me, and it seems that the least I can do is cooperate."

"Commendable." Gillespie smiled. "Ginny, is it possible that you're afraid to leave here? Are you afraid to go home, to go back to school? The idea has occurred to us."

Ginny remained calm; it was almost as if she had prepared herself for the accusation. "It isn't true," she said softly.

"If someone said that to me, I might protest a little more vigorously."

"I guess I'm not the excitable type," she said in the same soft voice.

Kildare, who was standing near the door, said, "Ginny,

you can blame this on me. From our talk yesterday, I got the idea that you're balking at returning to a situation where you won't be ... well, where you won't be the champion."

She looked at him but said nothing.

"Ginny, the mind is a fantastic mechanism," Gillespie said. "Unbelievable as it may seem, people can use their minds to create physical disabilities. And, in a sense, those disabilities actually exist. It's our opinion that, subconsciously, you have created the factor that keeps you from using your hand."

She shook her head, still calm.

"I'm not accusing you of intentionally trying to deceive us. If our theory is right, you honestly believe that your hand is physically impaired. But that's only because you are subconsciously forcing yourself to believe it—and for a specific reason. The suggestion that Dr. Kildare made could very well be that reason. Is that not so?"

Ginny shook her head more emphatically—but still said nothing.

"I'll admit this," Gillespie went on, "we could be wrong. The trouble could actually be physical. That's why we're continuing with the examinations, looking for a cause. You said a moment ago that the least you could do was cooperate. All right, that's what I want you to do. Cooperate. We're assuming that you could be right—that's why we haven't called off the examinations. Do the same for us, assume that *we* could be correct. Ask yourself truthfully if it isn't possible that your problem is psychological, not physical."

Finally, she spoke. There was a core of steeliness in her tone. "You're wrong, Dr. Gillespie. You're so wrong. I admit that I want to stay here. But only because I want to get well. I don't want to be like this."

"Won't you give our theory a chance?"

"I can't. You're wrong. I can't use my hand. I try. I try, but I just can't. Believe me. Please believe me."

Gillespie got to his feet and began pacing, as earlier he had paced his own office. "Ginny, you're sixteen. In a few more years, you'll be of legal age—an adult. Seen from your standpoint now, adulthood is a time of privilege. What you may not realize is that it's more a time of responsibility. There is no reason why you should be completely ready for the responsibilities of adulthood right now—but you should be nearing that point. A person doesn't suddenly become responsible overnight when he reaches the legal age for it.

It's a gradual process, you know."

"Doctor—"

"Give me a second more," he said. "One of the more pleasurable, but at the same time burdensome, responsibilities of adulthood is independence. You're going to find in a few years that you're no longer George and Mary Dugan's daughter—that you're Ginny Dugan, individual. At that time, you'll have to stop being what your mother wants you to be, or what your father wants you to be—you'll have to function according to those forces within your own mind and your own soul which are you. I say that you'll *have* to. But, of course, that isn't entirely true. Some people never make the break from dependence to independence. They go through life blindly doing what is expected of them by others. But they're not individuals within themselves, they're reflections of other individuals. Am I making myself clear?"

"Yes, but—"

"Don't imagine that I'm telling you to denounce your parents. I'm not. What I'm saying is that you have to start now to prepare yourself for another time, a time when you'll be on your own." He halted the pacing. "Have you thought about the future—your future—at all?"

"Of course. Everyone does."

"This baton twirling. Dr. Kildare tells me that it provides you with a certain prominence, makes you a certain celebrity among your friends. He believes, as he explained a second ago, that it has become so important to you that you resist returning to a situation where it no longer exists. May I ask you this? How long did you expect your baton twirling to continue? Past high school? Past college? On into adulthood? Hasn't it occurred to you that eventually it had to end?"

Her eyes opened wide and she stared at him as if he had abruptly reached out and slapped her.

"It's time for you to be what you are, Ginny," Gillespie said. "Don't be a prisoner of what you can do."

Tears brimmed in her eyes. "What am I, Doctor? When I lost what I could do, I lost my friends."

"If that's true, then they weren't friends, they were hangers-on. But I doubt very much that it is true. I suspect that you didn't lose your friends, that you drove them away —out of fear. The fear that you didn't really deserve them, or the fear that they were going to desert you. Could that be it? Was it because you thought they were going to leave you and you wanted to save face, to get in the first blow?"

"No!" she suddenly shouted. "No, that's not true!"

"Well, you should know. But I wonder if you do." He shook his head sadly. "I wonder." He approached her chair. "Ginny, I think Dr. Kildare is right. To you, this hospital is a place to hide. But you can't hide forever. There has to be a day of reckoning, a time to leave. How do you want to go? As a frightened child? Or as a girl who's ready to be an adult?"

"You're wrong!" she screamed. "You're wrong! Listen to me! Listen! I'm not afraid! It's my hand, my hand! Doctor, believe me. Please! Please believe me!"

Gillespie turned and headed for the door. "Kildare."

Kildare followed him out. In the corridor, they halted. Kildare looked at Gillespie disapprovingly.

"You think I was too tough on her."

"We might be wrong," Kildare said. "Suppose we are? Suppose there is a physical cause?"

"Then I'll apologize."

"You hit her pretty hard."

"If we're right, she needed it. If we're wrong . . . well,

she'll survive. I think your Ginny Dugan has some tough-
ness of her own." He walked on and Kildare accompanied
him. "I want her released as soon as possible," Gillespie said.
"Nothing is being gained by keeping her here."

"You mean stop the examinations?"

"No. Unless she brings herself to admit that the trouble
is psychological, we'll have to keep looking for the physical
cause. But she doesn't have to stay here. Send her home;
send her back to school. We can schedule the examinations
for after classes."

"Yes, we can do that. But I have a number of examinations already on the schedule. Shall I hold her here for
those?"

"How long will it be?"

"A couple days."

"All right, I'm agreeable to that. But no longer. Make
sure of that."

They reached the elevators and halted again and Gillespie punched the button. "I'll say to you what I said to her,"
he said to Kildare. "She can't hide here."

Kildare nodded.

Then the elevator door opened and Gillespie got aboard.

In the Dugan home, George and Mary Dugan sat across from each other at the breakfast table. It was after ten o'clock. They both had their eyes on their food and they were eating as if it had a bad taste.

"Aren't you going to the office at all today?" Mary said.

"I may and I may not," George said gruffly. "I think I deserve a day off. How often do I stay away?"

"That's what worries me. This is so unusual."

George pushed his plate away and got up and went into the living room. Mary sat for another minute or so, then she arose and followed him. He was sitting in a chair, facing a window, with his big hands locked together under his chin.

"Do you want a doctor?"

He looked at her for an instant, then turned away again. "No, I don't want a doctor. I'm fine. There's nothing wrong with me. I want a day off, that's all. Is that a crime?"

She sat down at one end of the couch. "You didn't sleep last night."

"How do you know?"

"I didn't sleep either."

He shrugged. "Probably those spareribs we had for

dinner. You made the sauce too spicy."

"You've never complained about it before."

"I'm not complaining now; I'm just saying." He got up and went to the television. "What's on at this time of day? That soap opera junk, I suppose."

"I wouldn't know. I never watch it in the morning."

A program came on and he watched it for a minute, then he switched off the set. "That's why you women never get anything done; you waste your time on that junk."

"I don't—" She let the protest die. "Do you want to know why I couldn't sleep?" she said.

"Those spareribs."

She shook her head. "No. I was thinking about Ginny."

"She'll be all right," he said, returning to the chair.

"Actually, I was thinking about what Dr. Kildare said about her and about us—you and me."

George sat up. "Now, listen—"

He was interrupted by the sound of the telephone ringing in the kitchen. "There's the phone."

"I heard it," Mary said. "It's probably your office calling."

"You answer it. Tell them to handle it themselves, whatever it is. I don't want to think about that now."

The phone rang again. Mary got up and headed for the kitchen. It rang the third time before she reached it.

George could hear his wife's voice as she spoke on the phone, but he could not make out her words. He scowled. "Tell them I'm taking the day off and that's that," he called to her. She did not answer. Then he heard her hang up, and a second later she reappeared in the living room.

"That was Dr. Kildare," she said. Her voice trembled. "He's going to release Ginny on Saturday."

George grunted.

"On Saturday," Mary said. "That's the day of the contest."

George swung around and looked at her. "I don't suppose he said they'd fixed up her hand."

"No. They're going to send her home, and then they're going to arrange for her to take the rest of the examinations after classes."

"Oh boy, they're really trying to weasel out." He shook a finger. "But they're not going to get away with it. I'm going to see a lawyer."

Mary sat down. She covered her face with her hands and began to cry. "George," she said through the tears, "he's right, isn't he?" She didn't look up.

"Right? Right? Who's right? Right about what?"

"Dr. Kildare. He's right about Ginny and us. I was awake all night thinking about it. And I can't deny it any longer. He *is* right. I made baton twirling seem too important. I don't know why I did. I just . . . it *seemed* important to me. I wanted her to have friends, and. . . ." She began to weep harder. "I don't know. I just don't know."

George got up and went to her and put an arm around her. "Honey, don't blame yourself. Sure, you pushed that baton business too hard, but that has nothing to do with what's happened. That's crazy."

"He was right about you, too," she wept. "You never even try to realize that Ginny is a girl and that she doesn't think the way you do or want the things you want."

"Well, maybe I'm kind of stiff, but you know me. It's all sound."

"She doesn't understand that."

"It's about time she did."

"Why? Why is it that everyone else always has to do the understanding?"

"Because—" He got up and went to the windows. "I don't know," he said, standing with his back to her. "It's just my way."

"Would you accept that excuse from Ginny?"

"Now look—"

"George, don't fight me. This is important. I've been pushing Ginny and you've been pulling her; it's no wonder she's confused."

"All right, I'll admit it, she's confused. And maybe we're at fault. So where do we go from here? Is it going to fix up her hand? No. The one thing doesn't have anything to do with the other. They're separate. You can't make me believe that because I've been a little rough on Ginny that that's why she can't use her hand. It doesn't make sense."

"George, not everything does make sense—at least, not to every person. But this, it makes sense to Dr. Kildare. And he knows about—"

George whipped around and waggled a finger at her. "He's trying to weasel out."

"There's probably something about your business that wouldn't make sense to him. But that doesn't mean that it's wrong. And I don't think that he would tell you flatly that it didn't make sense, that you were wrong, just because he didn't understand it."

"I tell you, he's trying to weasel out." He strode across the room. "I'm going to see a lawyer. I'm not going to take this lying down."

Mary sat and listened and heard him slam out the back door. Then she heard the car starting. She felt defeated. With him gone, there was only one way to strike back. "Lying down," she murmured, correcting his grammar. But the effect was far from satisfying.

As for George, he changed his mind about going to see his lawyer. Halfway there, he turned off and went to his own office. When he arrived, he stopped at the receptionist's desk and bawled her out for an error she had committed three days earlier. Then he went to his private office and slumped down in his swivel chair and stared gloomily at the work on his desk. Five minutes later, he arose and returned to the receptionist's desk and apologized. But even after that he was still unsatisfied.

11 "We Found the Unknown!"

On Saturday morning, Kildare went to Ginny's room. She was sitting on the edge of her bed. He motioned to her and said, "Come with me." His manner was pleasant enough.

"Another examination?" she asked. "I don't know why you keep it up if you don't believe me."

Kildare made no comment. He opened the door and stood back for her to pass. He followed her out and led the way down the corridor.

At the elevators, he said, "This is the day of the contest, isn't it?"

"Yes." There was a tautness in her tone.

"You're not going?"

"No."

The elevator arrived and they boarded. As it descended, Kildare said, "Your parents will be here soon. There would be time for you to get to the contest."

"Dr. Kildare, I *know* that."

At the second floor, they left the car. With Kildare still leading, they entered a ward. Ginny hesitated, suddenly realizing that this was where Mr. Morris and Mr. Grosvenor were quartered. But Kildare moved on, ignoring her hesitation, and she had no choice but to hustle to catch up to him.

Kildare halted in the aisle between Mr. Grosvenor's and Mr. Morris's beds. Ginny drew up behind him.

Seeing Ginny, both men smiled. Morris added a wink to his smile. But Grosvenor was now incapable of offering anything extra; he was even paler than before and it was clear that he had very little strength left in his body.

Ginny was shocked by Grosvenor's appearance. She had

not realized the acuteness of his illness. Tears moistened her eyes and she reached out and put a sympathetic hand on his arm, as if hoping that her touch would put life back into him.

"Ginny is leaving us today," Kildare said. "She wanted to say good-bye."

She nodded feebly. "Yes . . . yes, I wanted to say good-bye."

Morris turned to his friend. "Ginny's going home today," he said. "She stopped to say good-bye."

"I heard, I heard," Grosvenor replied grumpily. His voice was little more than a whisper, but it still had spirit.

"Grosvenor don't hear so well anymore," Morris said to Ginny, smiling.

"I got the ears of a boy of twenty," Grosvenor said. "The trouble is, nobody speaks up anymore these days. A bunch of whisperers."

"He hears so bad, we had to give up the checker game," Morris said. "He couldn't hear me when I told him where to move."

"But he was the one who used to tell you where to move," Ginny said.

"The shoe changed over to the other foot. When it got so I had a thousand games to the better of him, he decided to take advice instead of give it. But even getting, that didn't help him neither. We called it quits when I got so far ahead that we couldn't work with the astronomical figures it took to measure how much I was to the good."

Grosvenor shook his head weakly. "The good Lord forgive you, Morris, for the tales you tell."

"Grosvenor missed you," Morris said. "We thought you'd gone home. So we asked Dr. Kildare here about you. Without your goodness of the heart to back him up, Grosvenor couldn't win no arguments."

"It was Morris asked about you," Grosvenor said.

"As I recall, it was Grosvenor," Morris said. "Exactly and specifically, he said to me, 'Where's that Ginny? She don't come around anymore. Has she gone home?' That's what he said. I remember the exact words."

"You should—you said them," Grosvenor said.

Kildare smiled. "We better be going," he said. Then he explained to the men, "Ginny's parents are coming to pick her up."

Ginny patted Grosvenor's arm. "Good-bye. . . ." Then

she turned to Morris. "Good-bye, Mr. Morris."

Morris winked again. "Get some of that sunshine," he said.

Ginny and Kildare moved away toward the exit.

"Why did you bring me here?" Ginny asked. "How did you know that I used to . . . I mean that. . . ."

"How did I know that you used to referee the checker games? There aren't many secrets in a hospital."

They reached the elevator and waited for a car.

"Poor Mr. Grosvenor," Ginny said sadly. "I didn't realize. He was so—so chipper. Before, I mean. I thought. . . ." She sighed. "I don't know what I thought. But I didn't think this."

The elevator arrived and they boarded and ascended to Ginny's floor. Kildare gestured her out of the car, then walked beside her on the way back to her room.

"I didn't take you to Morris and Grosvenor just so you could say good-bye," he said. "I had another reason." He was silent for a second, then he said, "Do you want to know why they're here in the hospital?"

"Yes."

"Mr. Morris has a type of meningitis. Mr. Grosvenor has

leukemia, a type of cancer."

"Mr. Grosvenor looks so awful—so weak. It happened so fast."

"Yes, when leukemia hits, it hits hard and fast." He opened the door to Ginny's room for her to enter. "They're both dying," he said. "They were dying before, too, when you visited them. It's not something that's just happened today."

She halted and looked at him. "Mr. Morris, too? I assumed that Mr. Grosvenor was, but—but Mr. Morris. . . ."

"Yes, Mr. Morris, too."

Ginny moved on and went to the windows and stood facing away from Kildare.

"There is a remote possibility that Mr. Morris and Mr. Grosvenor may not die," Kildare said, sitting down in Ginny's chair. "But it's so remote that we don't even admit to ourselves that it exists. It depends on what is often called a miracle. The miracle is medical research. Hours of it, days of it, months of it, years of it. There are doctors working right now in this hospital trying to find the cures for Mr. Morris's meningitis and Mr. Grosvenor's leukemia. But it's not likely that they'll find the cures in time. It's possible that they'll never find them."

"I'm sorry," Ginny said miserably.

"It isn't your fault." Again, he was silent for a second, then he said, "I suppose you're wondering what this has to do with you."

"A little."

"A good many hours have been devoted to your examinations, Ginny. And there are many more hours to go yet, because we intend to keep looking for the physical cause that you say makes it impossible for you to use your hand. Those hours could be used for some other cause—for instance, for seeking the cure to some so far incurable disease. I want you to be aware of that."

He waited for a word of response. But the only sign was a gradual stiffening of her body, which could have meant anything.

"Dr. Gillespie said that you're hiding, Ginny. If he was right, you're not hiding from any threat from the outside. It's because of a fear that's within yourself." He got to his feet. "When do you plan to start fighting the fear? Tomorrow? The next day? Is that what you tell yourself—that you'll be strong tomorrow? That kind of tomorrow never comes." He went to the door. "It's up to you, Ginny. You can leave here frightened, or you can leave here unafraid."

A small sound that might have been a sob came from her. Kildare left and closed the door softly behind him.

For a long, long moment, Ginny did not move. Then she turned and faced the room. Tears were trickling down her cheeks. She held back for another instant. Then she walked to the small metal stand that was beside her bed and stared at the rubber ball that was resting there. After another moment of anguished hesitation she reached out with her left hand and picked up the ball and placed it in the palm of her right hand.

The tears stopped. She concentrated her attention fully on the rubber ball. It seemed suddenly large—as large as her fear. Suppose Dr. Kildare was wrong? She was afraid now to try to close her hand, afraid of what she might discover. Then she thought again about Mr. Morris and Mr. Grosvenor. She thought about what they were facing, and about how they were facing it.

Slowly, her fingers curled. They trembled. Ginny began to weep again as she saw the movement of the fingers and realized that they were responding to the force of her own will. Then the fingers closed on the ball—not tightly, but they *did* close. A small cry escaped from Ginny, a sound that was a mixture of relief and shame. Then, still clutching the ball, she threw herself across the bed and wept from deep in her soul, wept for joy and for sorrow, wept for herself and for Mr. Morris and for Mr. Grosvenor.

The Dugans arrived at the hospital a little before noon. The nurse at the charge desk called Dr. Kildare to get his authorization for Ginny's release. When he reached the desk, the Dugans were standing by; George glowering, Mary with her eyes averted.

Kildare smiled genially. "Good morning."

Mary nodded and George said gruffly, "Hiya."

Kildare signed the authorization, then turned again to the Dugans. "I've made all the arrangements for Ginny to continue the examinations after classes," he said. "You'll receive a notice in the mail each time a test is scheduled. It will give the date and time."

"Yeah, well, if you think this is the end of it, you're sadly mistaken," George said. "The first thing Monday, I'm going to see a lawyer. You may think you can kick us

out and be done with it, but you've got a responsibility and I'm going to see that you honor it."

Kildare looked at him evenly. "Mr. Dugan, we intend to continue the examinations, I told you that."

"When? When you happen to get bored around here doing nothing and happen to want to get in a little practice at being a stage-show psychiatrist? Is that when? And I guess even that won't last very long, will it? Maybe we'll get a couple of notices, but after that, I guess we won't hear much from you. Throw 'em a few crumbs, that's the old system—right?"

"George, please," Mary said.

"Please what? They've made a cripple out of my daughter. What am I supposed to do, just take it? What do you want me to do, be a gentleman? Do you want me to say, 'Oh, that's okay, boys, everybody makes mistakes.' Is that what you want? Well, no thanks!"

"Mr. Dugan," Kildare said, holding fast to his temper, "we have no intention of abandoning your daughter. I told you that we will continue the examinations, and we will. But there is no point in her staying here. She should be home; she should be in school."

"Uh-huh. Yeah. Words. I know a fast shuffle when I see it. Where she belongs is here. Right here where the goof-up happened. Right here where you can keep at it day and night, looking for where you went wrong."

"That isn't the way it works," Kildare said. "Evaluations have to be made between examinations. It takes time."

"We'll see what the law says," George snapped. "When my lawyer gets through with you people here, you'll be singing a different tune."

Woodenly, Kildare said, "It's the privilege of every citizen to seek recourse through the law."

"You won't be so cocky when I get damages."

Kildare nodded. "Mr. Dugan, I have one more thing to say. It is my duty to suggest to you that you arrange for psychiatric care for your daughter. This is a professional opinion. It's our belief—not only my belief, but the Medical Director's belief, too—that Ginny's trouble is psychological. I explained that to you the other day. Now, as I say, that's a professional opinion. You can act on it or not. The responsibility is yours."

"I told you what I'm going to do."

Kildare lifted his hands in defeat. "Then it's pointless

for me to say anymore." He headed down the corridor toward Ginny's room. "Come along, we'll see if your daughter is ready to leave."

The Dugans followed him; George muttering under his breath, Mary saying nothing.

When they reached the room, they found Ginny standing at one of the windows, dressed to leave. She turned to face them as they entered.

"You're a little early," she said listlessly. "I wasn't expecting you yet."

"We figured we might as well come along," George said. "No sense in waiting."

Mary went to her. "Where are your things, dear? And, heavens, look at your hair! You can't go out looking like that. Sit down over here," she said, indicating one of the chairs. "I'll just go over your hair a bit with a comb."

Ginny sat down and Mary took a comb from her purse and began pulling it through Ginny's hair. Ginny looked straight at Kildare. He smiled, then went to the easy chair and sat down.

"Can't you hurry it up?" George said irritably to his wife. He moved restlessly around the room.

"Get Ginny's things together, dear," she replied.

"They're all packed," Ginny said. "They're in the suitcase there by the bed."

Mary finished the combing. "That's better." She smiled nervously at her husband. "Well. . . ."

George picked up the suitcase. "I guess we can go." He turned to Kildare. "You'll be hearing from me."

"Wait," Mary said. "Ginny's baton and her costumes." To Ginny, she said, "Where are they, dear?"

Ginny paled. "In the closet," she said, her voice faint.

"I'll get them," Mary said, heading toward the closet.

"No!" Ginny suddenly shouted.

They all faced her.

Ginny burst into sobs. She ran to her mother and clung to her. Mary held her and patted her. "Darling, what's the matter? What's wrong?"

"My hand," Ginny wept. "I *can* use it. I can. I'm sorry. Please forgive me. I'm sorry. I didn't know. Look!" She lifted her arm and the fingers curled and then straightened. She wept convulsively, clinging fiercely to her mother.

Mary began to cry, too. "It's all right, dear. It's all right."

George took in a deep breath and let it out slowly, as if

it were his last one. He went to the bed and sat down heavily. His whole body sagged. He kept his eyes lowered to hide his own tears.

"If you want an outsider's opinion," Kildare said, "this is hardly the time for weeping. The pain is ended."

George looked up. "I owe you a pretty big apology."

"It isn't necessary."

George looked down again. "I spend half my life apologizing."

"You might try understanding first," Kildare suggested. "I have an idea that might eliminate the problem."

George nodded.

Ginny broke away from her mother. She was trembling, trying to stop her tears. "Dr. Kildare, I didn't lie to you," she said. "I couldn't use my hand. I really couldn't. Until today."

"I believe you."

"I don't understand it. Or maybe I do. I don't know. I— I thought about what you said—about Mr. Morris and Mr. Grosvenor—I thought about that, and then I picked up that rubber ball and put it in my hand, and—and my fingers worked. Not as well as they used to, but. . . ." She went to the stand and picked up the ball with her right hand. "See? I can really close my fingers."

"It will improve," Kildare said. "You're out of practice. The muscles are stiff from lack of use."

"But I still don't understand."

"You grew up a bit, got a bit closer to adulthood." Kildare smiled. "You saw that you had a responsibility not to take the time of the researchers, the doctors, if there was no real reason for it. You saw the responsibility, and you accepted it. And doing that made you less afraid of facing other responsibilities." He turned toward George Dugan. "Your parents will explain the rest of it," he said.

George straightened. "Yes," he said to Ginny, "we all have some talking, some explaining to do." Then he said to Kildare, "And this time, I'll do as you said—I'll do some listening along with the talking."

Mary put her arm around her daughter. "Let's go now. We have a lot to talk about." Then she headed for the closet again. "I'll get your—"

"Mother. . . ."

Mary halted.

"I'll get them," Ginny said. She went to the closet and

got out the baton and the overnight bag that held the costumes. She smiled at Kildare. "The pain is ended," she said. She held the baton in her right hand and said to her father, "It *is* just a stick, isn't it?"

George shook his head. "No, it's a baton, honey. And if you get some kind of pleasure out of throwing it—I mean, twirling it—then I guess. . . ." He grinned self-consciously. "Well, you know. . . ."

At that moment, the door opened. Bob Carmody appeared in the entrance. He smiled amiably. "Hi." Then he looked directly at Ginny, frowning. "I didn't know you were getting out today. The nurse just told me."

"Oh," she said.

"What I mean is, I thought that as long as you couldn't go to the contest— I mean, that was what I was thinking before. I was thinking that you might want some company."

"Thank you." Ginny smiled.

He looked from Ginny to Mrs. Dugan and then to Mr. Dugan. "But I guess you've got plenty of company."

George strode forward, grinning. "The more the merrier, Bob. In fact, I was just saying—thinking of saying, anyway—I was just saying, why don't we all go to the contest? Can we still make it?" He halted and turned to Ginny. "You want to go, don't you, honey?"

"I want to go," she said.

"Well, what are we waiting for?" He made gathering motions with his hands. "Come on, family. Before I change my mind." He winked at Ginny. "I can think of lots better things to do than watching a bunch of kids throwing a bunch of sticks around."

Ginny laughed. Then they all went out into the hall.

George was the last in line and he stopped and turned back to Kildare. "I guess I made a monkey of myself," he said. "It's my way, you might say. More often than not, I have to play the monkey before I see the sense of things. But maybe I can change—a little, anyway—if I try. If I do, I want to say that you can take the credit for it."

"Don't change too much," Kildare warned. "One extreme is as bad as another."

"At my age, a man doesn't do a complete turnabout, so I guess there's no worry on that count." He put out a hand. "Thank you, Doctor."

Kildare shook the hand. "My pleasure."

They walked together to the charge desk; then Kildare halted and George went on alone to the elevators where the others were waiting. Kildare watched them, smiling to himself.

The elevator door opened and they stepped aboard. But then Ginny got out and walked back to where Kildare was standing, letting the car go on without her.

When she reached him, she said, "I told them I'd catch up. I wanted to tell you that I'll be coming back. I'll be back tomorrow."

"Not as a patient, I hope."

"No. As a—well, I don't know what you'd call it. I'd like to come back and visit with Mr. Morris and Mr. Grosvenor—if that's permitted."

"It is. And I think they'd like it."

"I thought that maybe we could get the checkers game going again. They could tell me where they want the checkers moved and I could move them."

"That's a good idea. The whole ward misses that checkers game."

"I owe them a great deal, Doctor. I think that now I can be what you and Dr. Gillespie said I should be—myself. I want to do something to repay all of you."

"There is one thing you can do." Kildare smiled. "You can go to that contest and cheer for Ellen Morley."

"I'd planned to do that. And I'll mean it."

"Then we're even," Kildare said.

"Good-bye, Doctor—for now."

"Good-bye, Ginny."

He watched her walk back to the elevators, wait, and then get aboard a car.

Dr. Everleigh came around a corner and headed in Kildare's direction. He was carrying a clipboard, studying whatever information was on it, and not looking where he was going.

As Everleigh reached the charge desk, Kildare spoke to him. "The Dugan girl just checked out," he said.

Everleigh stopped and looked at Kildare blankly.

"Ginny Dugan just checked out," Kildare said again. "We found the 'unknown.'"

"Fine," Everleigh said, preoccupied. He tapped the clipboard with a finger. "Look, Jim, I've got a patient here who's clotting and there doesn't seem to be any logical reason for it. I'm transfusing with whole blood. I've given him injections of dicoumarol. . . ."

The two doctors stood discussing the perplexity for another few minutes, then they walked on down the corridor together, still talking, wholly absorbed with a new unknown.

Whitman CLASSICS

Five Little Peppers Midway	Little Men
Freckles	Five Little Peppers and How They Grew
Wild Animals I Have Known	Robinson Crusoe
Rebecca of Sunnybrook Farm	Treasure Island
Alice in Wonderland	Heidi
Mrs. Wiggs of the Cabbage Patch	The Call of the Wild
Fifty Famous Fairy Tales	Tom Sawyer
Rose in Bloom	Beautiful Joe
Eight Cousins	Adventures of Sherlock Holmes
Little Women	

Here are some of the best-loved stories of all time. Delightful ... intriguing ... never-to-be-forgotten tales that you will read again and again. Start your own home library of WHITMAN CLASSICS so that you'll always have exciting books at your finger tips.

Whitman

REG. U.S. PAT. OFF.

Whitman ADVENTURE and MYSTERY Books

Adventure Stories for GIRLS and BOYS...

TIMBER TRAIL RIDERS

The Long Trail North
The Texas Tenderfoot
The Luck of Black Diamond

THE BOBBSEY TWINS

In the Country
Merry Days Indoors and Out
At the Seashore

DONNA PARKER

In Hollywood
At Cherrydale
Special Agent
On Her Own
A Spring to Remember
Mystery at Arawak

TROY NESBIT SERIES

The Forest Fire Mystery
The Jinx of Payrock Canyon
Sand Dune Pony

New Stories About Your Television Favorites...

Dr. Kildare
Assigned to Trouble

Janet Lennon
And the Angels
Adventure at Two Rivers
Camp Calamity

Walt Disney's Annette
The Mystery at Smugglers' Cove
The Desert Inn Mystery
Sierra Summer
The Mystery at Moonstone Bay

The Lennon Sisters
Secret of Holiday Island

Leave It to Beaver

Ripcord

The Beverly Hillbillies

Lassie
The Mystery at Blackberry Bog

Lucy
The Madcap Mystery